# THE DAUGHTER IN LIMBO

## By George O. Otiono

Copyright © 2015 George O. Otiono

All Rights Reserved

Printed in the United States of America

ISBN: 978-0-9985915-2-0

For permission to reproduce selections in this book or for information about this book, write to *stories@dzous.com*

Cover art: Hieronymus Bosch

DZOUS

Sacramento

--To George, Calvin, and Brando for their love and support.

--To Erica for the love, support and peaceful demeanor that gave me the space to immerse myself in an imaginary world long enough to write this novel.

Every wrongdoing that God despises
Results in an injury, and each of such injuries
Either by force or fraud causes pain and distress to other people.
--Dante Alighieri, *Inferno*

# CHAPTER 1

The thought that tomorrow, less than seven hours away, was the day of the visit nagged Elizabeth Egi Kōp that night like a mild headache.

Yet several weeks ago, the whole thing had started with her smiling twice as Don tried to spin the web of seduction around her. At the time, on March 15 to be exact, while his body language tried to make her believe she was the most important person in the whole wide world—its queen—his smooth tongue had claimed that his relationship status was zero, nil, nonexistent—though she'd observed him driving a steady stream of girls apparently to his place. Yes, more than half the world would have called him a liar to his face or in their minds and sneered. She didn't. In fact, her face had crinkled into a smile as the delightful thought that she'd been right about him came to her. *He is a guy who dated for dating sake, an eligible bachelor frightened of getting tied down in a serious relationship, a you-stay-there-and-I-stay-here sort of man, a rolling stone.*

She'd paused for just a second to know how that played into her psyche, thinking: *No, dating can't be to satisfy just A or just B. It has to be about A and B. It must be a package of what I want and what I need.* She wanted a man to roll into her space occasionally. Being the odd woman out of the dating scene had started to impinge on her ego and a part of her kept telling her to live a little. At the ripe age of twenty-three, she had to heed that advice and unshackle herself for a taste of life. But she needed to do so with caution, with one foot in and the other foot out. Don or his type promised what she wanted and needed. Thus, her face had beamed with the full wattage smile that stretched her lips, twinkled her eyes and lit up the world.

She had jaunted off that day convinced that both of them had signed up for a casual affair. A few dates later, she remained sure she'd found the right man for her situation. The last time they met, however, he had shaken her faith in the arrangement. Don had invited her to a lunch date. She had asked, "When?"

"Next week," he had said.

"Which day?"

"I'm open all week—just come any day."

She had frowned. For the date, he hadn't offered one day, two days, or even three days—but an entire week. If a calendar for his dates existed, her name alone would scroll across five straight days of it. Such devotion of his time to one girl was totally out of character and quite unexpected. Anyone who knew him would have been startled to hear that he cleared his lunch calendar an entire week for a girl who really couldn't qualify as a fashionista in CDKuru. *I can't just blurt out my answer*, she had thought. *For some reason, he seems insecure. A negative answer might make him feel small, especially since I can't plead time constraint for refusing a weeklong open invitation.* Elizabeth had tried to dance around his request without hurting his feelings and had eventually left him with the ambiguous answer of "Let's see."

The week had come and gone without her being anywhere close to his office or to him. And for a time afterward she believed that since he didn't know where she lived and she wouldn't visit him that the whole affair had run its course so quickly, that they had parted forever. *Never the twain shall meet*, she smiled wryly as Rudyard Kipling's words slipped into her

6

head. *Oh. East is East, and West is West, and never the twain shall meet.*

But then bits and pieces of the episode began to float around in her head. *I told him, "Let's see." ... That can sound promising when you are hopeful. ... Hope makes people see only the bright side. And to hope for something and not get it hurts more. ... I must have bruised his ego.* She had begun to see herself as cruel. Yes, her goal had been to remain true to the terms of their relationship, but she could have still steered him gently, gently, to the idea that he should not devote too much time to her. There was no need to let him down roughly. Shame had unleashed its pain on her. She felt it especially in the pit of her stomach and died a little. "I will just make up for the lunch date by visiting him tomorrow," she had muttered and had escaped the ill feeling.

Tonight she couldn't sleep. The megalopolis of CDKuru had gone to bed at its usual hour, around nine. Towering metal gates—anchored to prison-high walls to protect individual houses, residential streets and residential neighborhoods—had virtually all clanged shut. The city's daily din had died out, leaving the place in deep silence. Now, blinding darkness entombed most parts of the megacity, especially low-rent areas where residents had to choose between skimpy meals and meager electricity from tiny generators. Residents of the row of small rooming houses in the front part of Irnopi slum had chosen skimpy meals and so the area remained buried in pitch-black mound of nightfall.

The second house on that row was about 760 square feet of eleven compartments: eight bedrooms, a communal "bathroom," a communal toilet, and a kitchenette area. The bedrooms—four on each side of a three-foot wide common corridor—faced each other. Two of the rooms had quite a cachet in the compound. Both had a connecting door that made them a rental unit. Each of the other rooms there was a single unit with four solid walls and a door to the corridor. The special unit belonged to Elizabeth's uncle who along with his wife and their oldest daughter slept in the inner room, while Elizabeth and three of the couple's younger children squeezed into the other room— the children on the floor, she on the only bed in that room.

The dire thought that the visit won't go well kept intruding into her mind, though she had yet to conceive one or more specific scenarios of what might go wrong. Would she trip and fall in his crowded reception room? Would he scream and shame her? ... She did not pinpoint or try to pinpoint one such potential incident and so the thread of unease looped around and around in her mind. She began to distract herself by etching the details of the night in her memory. Every sound in the rooms cut through the tar-black darkness to her ears. Mosquito or mosquitoes (she couldn't tell how many) circled her ears, whining and warning her to expect some bites imminently. She swatted randomly at the invisible insect or insects and ended up slapping herself several times on the neck and face. Intermittently, a cacophony of snores issued from the kids sleeping on the mat—snores from drawn-out wheezing to guttural sounds.

Then whispers came from the other room to subsume the sounds in her room. *What do I do now? I don't want to hear their discussion, yet I still don't want to think about tomorrow.* Her ploy for escaping intrusive thoughts had run into trouble. The ploy required her to keep her mind busy with benign thoughts. "An idle mind is the devil's workshop," she'd heard. She couldn't work, work, work to keep her mind from being idle. She wasn't in an open field, an office or a classroom—she was in an overcrowded bedroom near midnight. So she had listened hard, ears hustling as if every sound in there carried the secret of everlasting life, and streamed the details of her milieu in her mind. Now, if she continued to listen, she would hear what she didn't want to hear. If she stopped listening, she would start thinking about something she didn't want to think about. Trapped in her dilemma, she did nothing and the primary sound in the room came through.

"What did you say?" he was saying.

"Her unfortunate father," the wife whispered. "That death."

The words echoed in Elizabeth's eardrums. She tuned out, trying to keep the words from getting into her brain, trying to quarantine them in the void between the ear and the brain until they lost their power to mean anything to her. Too late. The words ignited with meaning in her mind—and did more. Her imagination ran wild and filled up with a figment of blood pumping onto the concrete floor of a portico and rising into a flood. A bolt of panic shot through her, giving her an instant fever. Her body boiled and the breath in her lungs and chest turned to fumes. She felt weird and woozy and had her eyes flick open. Instead of the darkness in the room jamming into her eyeballs, a crimson film altered her vision. She screwed her eyes shut and instinctively heaved audibly—so audibly in fact that she thought the couple in the next room heard her. Nothing came from them.

*Tomorrow will not be a good day. Tomorrow will not be*

9

*a good day*, she thought insistently to distract herself from her emotional distress. Slowly the thought took hold, displacing the haunting imagery of minutes ago. Minutes later, she was remembering how her relationship with Don had rolled along and gathered moss.

She had met him at National Natural Resources Corporation where an elderly guard told her, "If you want anything done here for you without getting a headache, go to Mr. Don Ihoeyno."

"The MD?" Elizabeth had asked then, thinking that only the managing director had that last name in that corporation.

"Noooo!" the man had said in a shocked tone, before whispering: "His son. He is different."

At the time, Elizabeth was in "sub-retailing," meaning she collected a few clothes from retailers and sold them in offices to the few who supposedly had money for her merchandise. Selling to females had its headaches—many continually tried to buy on credit and most haggled every price all day long. The men didn't haggle much or seek to buy on credit—the problem was that many of them had to try their crude advances on her. The trade with Don was different. He paid full price and didn't bother her with anything. In fact, her first sale to him had been overpriced. She had quoted a price, expecting him—like the other men—to lob off ten to fifteen percent in one short statement. He paid the extravagant price. When she tried to refund the excess, he insisted she kept it. Later, as one thing led to another, he would learn that her job applications in different offices hadn't found the right person to push them along. "Don't worry," he had said. "I'm your guy here."

Again, one thing led to another until that March 15 day.

10

And there they were in an affair. Then, of course, he had spooked her. Lunch any day of the week, he had said. Just come any day. Why would a real ladies' man suddenly sacrifice the attention of hordes of women for that of one female? She wasn't his wife or his fiancée. Girlfriend? Well, you had to unpack that word to determine if it captured her place in that affair. Why would a moth cease flying towards light? Why would a bee cease flying towards honey? Why? She had no answer. But she knew what she didn't want. *He'd better not be angling for us to become a couple.* The thought alone drew cold sweat to her forehead.

With a small damp towel, Elizabeth mopped sweat from her forehead and neck. Though her nose picked up a whiff of musty odor from the towel—the odor of a towel that had been damp a little too long—she continued to dab herself with it because she preferred feeling a little dirty to squirming in layers of sweat. An invisible fire seemed to burn in the room and elsewhere. Geography and human beings had conspired to create heat that scorched like that of the convection oven and suffocated neophytes in such a way that they became hysterical. Geography had offered humid tropical lowlands; humans had built houses to have successive thick concrete walls. Between Elizabeth and the thoroughfare twelve feet away were walls, walls, walls—the room's four sturdy walls, the house's concrete ramparts high to the corrugated zinc roof, the continuum of ramparts of all houses on that row, and the gated monumental walls that barricaded the slum.

Not only did these successive thick walls around such tiny quarters impede airflow, they trapped the worst heat of that sweltering place inside the rooms. Hot, humid air stoked the room now that power outage had stilled the fan, and she felt hot vapors besieging her, wringing her scalp and tender upper body for as much sweat as possible. With the room burning up and her inside a little disturbed, Elizabeth could only catnap that night.

#

In the morning she splayed out, exhausted in bed long after she should have been up. The uncle had gone to work, the children had gone to school, and the uncle's wife had made two trips to the kitchenette area for house chores. Upon return to the room, with washed plates in hand, the woman said, "I thought you were going out. Or are you not well?" That prompted Elizabeth to drag herself out of bed to get ready. She went to bathe in the stall known in that part of the city as a bathroom—a tiny enclosure with concrete floor, a hole on the wall for drainage, and nothing else. To wash yourself there, you had to bring your own bucket of water. She had her own bucket of water. In the course of her bucket bath, after soaping herself, something from last night's figment slipped into her mind. For a second the scoop of water about to pour on her body acquired a crimson hue. She perused it. It was not blood, not even muddy water—just clear water.

When she got back to the dingy room and stood in front of the wall-anchored standing mirror, she realized that the bath had failed to rejuvenate her. She had no zest, a 60 on a scale of 100. She stared at her shadow in the mirror for a second before pulling the curtain a little to the side to allow in more of the weak morning light. Her image in the mirror brightened. Days ago, when she last saw herself in the mirror, she was in negligee and was every bit a chocolate voluptuous beauty in her early twenties. Now she looked as she felt: dull. Then inspiration struck. *I have to dress appropriately for the occasion,* she told herself. *I have to look the part.* She packed her braids into a frumpy high bun to mute the beauty that had keyed a million and one compliments. Presto! The allure of her dimpled cheeks, sumptuous lips, and dewy eyes on soft light brown face became no match for the dowdy hairstyle that was better suited to staying in bed than to outing.

*Now, where's that dress?* It was in the wardrobe. To fetch it, she maneuvered through the 56-square-foot room crammed with the bed, white refrigerator, standing fan, olive-green settee, small portable garment rack with cover and small coffee table that was set atop the settee last night but was now back to its daytime spot on the floor. She dressed. Out of habit, she drifted toward the mirror to give herself the usual appraisal.

The dress itself looked like a bad imitation of the nun's tunic—a faded gray chiffon gown so drab and oversized and droopy to the ankle as to make even Aphrodite or Venus look more asexual than a nun. *I have to wear it. I have to look like a toad today.* She halted her drift toward the mirror—she couldn't present herself to the mirror looking like a toad. You look in the mirror to accent the positive, to appreciate your nice makeup, your nice wear, your nice physique. You don't look in the mirror to ensure you look pitiful. And she knew that if she saw herself in the mirror, she would be tempted to improve her look. She grabbed her bag and tarried to collect herself before leaving.

Mirror or no mirror, she'd forgotten that in crowded households lives crisscrossed and entwined like latticework. She couldn't just decide to don ugly clothes to go out without facing a critique. That critique came from Big Mama, the uncle's wife, who entered the room, pulled the curtain farther to let in more drab sunlight from the corridor, found Elizabeth loitering there, and saw the dress. The woman's eyes grew to the size of ping-pong balls as she gazed at the dress. In her forties, this woman in tie-dyed loose blouse and wrapper was six feet and plus-sized—but not plus-sized in any parts of the body that would cause a doctor to demur. She had a lustrous dark face of oblong shape, plump lips, round nose, and soft round eyes that were the size of eggs. Her hair was a full mat of interlocking small braids, gray along the hairline. The woman gently shook her head to disapprove the ugly voluminous gown.

"You are too young," she bemoaned quietly, "to be dressing like a widow still in mourning."

"I haven't married a man yet," Elizabeth tried to banter, "and he is already dead."

"We can't joke about this."

Elizabeth had hoped to play off the criticism of her clothes, but now that the gambit had failed, she still owed the old woman an explanation. Yet Elizabeth couldn't volunteer her real reason for wearing the dress because she hadn't informed the woman of the affair yet. So she said, "I am tired of men in this city."

Perhaps, the half-truth would be enough for Big Mama. After all, she did know that sugar daddies and lascivious young car-owners in CDKuru usually leered at Elizabeth's shapely beauty, drooled like boarding house teenage boys out on a social occasion, and clamored to pick her up. Yes, it was no news that these men (some of them green-toothed, python-headed or chimpanzee-shaped) had unwittingly caused the young woman to start favoring much looser gowns. But Big Mama's theatrically widened eyes, fully incredulous, shot down that explanation. "At least tie a belt over that sack," she advised.

"That will spoil my plan."

"You think this man has the brain of a raccoon?" Big Mama charged.

"Which man?" Elizabeth feigned ignorance.

"The one you are going to see."

Elizabeth's pretenses came undone. She croaked, "I am hoping he doesn't like what he sees today."

"Be careful," the old woman warned. "Nobody becomes ugly in weeks. If your heart is not set on him, then find a better way to let him know."

"No, no, no," Elizabeth protested. "You won't understand."

"You are not a mad woman—you didn't decide to wear what you are wearing for no reason. Just be careful. Just don't dig your ditch too deep."

Elizabeth swallowed hard, became mute, and left for her appointment.

# CHAPTER 2

Rainfalls and floods over decades had eroded the opposite sides and the back of Irnopi into immense gullies. Even with mounds of garbage and waste in each gully, each was still deeper than nineteen feet. As such, Irnopi—a narrow, oblong pocket of ramshackle houses—had three inaccessible borders. Its boundary in front adjoined the service lane of W Avenue, the busy thoroughfare to many parts of the city and to two nearby national monuments, Lanoitan Theatre and Lanoitan Stadium. Directly opposite the slum, an exclusive shopping center dazzled on the other side of W Avenue; adjacent, after the slum's northern gully, Akala estate displayed attractive terraced duplexes and gorgeous homes in a serene setting with wide, tarred roads (wide, tarred but potholed roads).

As things were, a narrow dirt track under the shadow of a decrepit three-story building right outside the slum provided Irnopi's lone access to the thoroughfare, to the outside world. Residents who lived near the road were lucky. Those who lived in the first and only row of houses in the place were especially lucky because a narrower dirt track in front of their houses crossed the other one. Other residents had to demonstrate their triple jumping abilities to get to the outside world. In their way, gutters opened up with slush every few feet along a myriad of tight pedestrian trails that weaved between compounds in the slum's jungle part, where small houses packed tightly and faced many different directions to squeeze into available land. Hence those residents had to test the springs in their legs by hopping, skipping, and jumping toward W Avenue. Luckily for Elizabeth, she didn't have to do all that to get to the road to the thoroughfare, for her house was among those in the only row of houses in Irnopi.

Yet once her feet touched the rough, pothole-strewn road on her way to the bus stop, she knew that this was going to be a difficult visit. The usual apology that she would make just for the sake of peace belonged to a different time and place. Not today, not in his office. *I must not apologize no matter how wounded he looks or how contrite I feel. To apologize would be to cloud our situation.* She felt bad about the whole thing again. A list of what she should have, could have, and would have done streamed into her mind: She should have visited him early one day that week to make excuses for the latter lunch; she could have … Doubts about making the visit crept into her mind. Her footsteps flagged. *I should walk away. End the whole affair now. He can't find me.* Her feet crawled to a stop. *No! I can't be so unfair to him.*

Still she needed to prod herself to continue the journey. She got her hand feeling the outside of her bag for something inside. She felt it. It was the notebook. She pictured it in her mind. Half-inch thick with beige sheets, the notebook had a soft cover of brownish red color worn with age. Its content was in two parts: the first part consisted of pieces of her dead father's oration, and the second part was full of her incomplete discourse on assorted issues. Her love for her father imbued the notebook with the power of talisman, and part of its therapeutic value came from reminding her of him and by extension of their time together.

She remembered her father and immersed herself in the memory of a continual childhood activity in which she was his scribe and student. "I am Socrates," the father would say. "You are Plato." Some would say the man had no outlet for his extensive liberal education—so he unleashed it on his daughter. He would illuminate with quotations each topic that moved him at that particular moment; she would write on that notebook now ensconced in her bag. Though she started this in early elementary grades, she had to contend with spelling complex words phonetically. When her task as scribe was done, she became his student.

With her on his lap, he corrected her spelling errors, dissected words she'd identified for explanation so that she understood their general and contextual meanings, and summarized his dictated text in simple language. He always ended up amused, saying: "The difference between the wise and the knowledgeable is that one has digested complex ideas but the other has swallowed them whole." Then, dying with laughter, he would ask her to identify which group ended up constipated. She always joyfully gave him the obviously correct answer. *Ah! Those were the days!* She smiled to herself and her communion with the good old days helped Elizabeth escape her immediate concerns all the way to V Island to Don's inner office.

The office, located in a complex of office towers in the posh island, was rectangular and about five times the space of Elizabeth's Irnopi place. A suite, it had tan walls; two archways that marked out a lounge, business area and conference area; three bay windows; and wall-to-wall ivory carpet. In the lounge, a 50-inch wall-mounted television played satirical skits to ghosts on an ornate five-person sectional and on two armchairs that flanked three sides of a coffee table. No one also sat on any of the seven bulky chairs flanking an equally bulky table in the conference area at the end of the suite.

Only Don sat in the entire suite. Center stage, in an area with a galore of polished mahogany panels and cabinets vaulting to the sky-high ceiling, he sat on a wheeled swivel executive chair behind a U-shaped executive table with room to rove. A mahogany credenza with hutch loomed behind him. Five black guest seats on the outside of his table invited with leather so velvet-soft it had Elizabeth on her first contact with it, on her first visit, lost in the rapture of feeling the plush material with her palm. Amused then, Don had ridden his seat very close to the table to purr with a smile, "I-talian. People always do that."

Today she entered the office to see the lanky thirtyish man on his executive seat arrested far from the table. Trendy to the second, he'd been swept along by the day's fashion sensibilities that colors symbolized nothing; this day, he wore all black—suit, shirt and tie—an outfit the classical-minded would have reserved for a funeral. She advanced past the lounge and saw that he looked lost in something that banished even the ghost of a smile from his lips or warmth from his eyes. Wreathed in gloom, he couldn't say "welcome" or "hello" and his silence chilled the atmosphere there. She came deeper into the gloomy air around him.

"Hello, Don," she said to cut through his despair.

He looked up. He had a light-skinned face fresh as a kid's, high angular cheekbones, and small eyes that had turned sad. The nose, remarkably overhanging the face, had the bridge flattened at the sides and alae tucked so high into the face that his nostrils couldn't be seen at eye level. Though he had looked up, he hadn't followed up with anything. He sat where he was—distant from his table and his guest—and spoke not a word of response to her "hello." She sat down warily.

Then it came out of him. "You made me look like a fool, like an idiot. A job was also here for you that week."

"A job?" she asked in bewilderment. "What did I do? Please explain."

He hadn't explained, couldn't explain, though words spewed out of him as his mood swung from despair to anger and back. Eventually he caught the vein of a rant about her making him look stupid and ranted on and on about it. He mentioned something about his secretary before the hammer came down: "I can't help you anymore. Sorry. I just can't."

An eerie hush befell the room. She sat shell-shocked by the unexpected developments. For the last fifteen months, she had sought a job without success. She had abandoned her doctoral program to move to CDKuru to try her luck in the impossible labor market that had lasted twenty-three plus years. And here she was being told that she unexpectedly had a job within grasp and lost it.

#

To be near and yet so far cuts deepest into the psyche. A person on a team with a heartbreak loss in the finals will have a vivid and concrete sense of losing the cup that a person on a non-playoff team will not have. A famished person staring at a feast through the window will have his or her hunger pangs sharpened and made even more acute. Greek gods, whose expertise in the sly use of hope gave us the word *tantalize*, understood the power of having someone's goal near enough to excite his or her senses and yet too far to reach. They put water and fruits within reach of Tantalus, but ensured that the nourishments always stayed just inches away from his hungry and thirsty mouth. Earlier on in CDKuru, once Elizabeth understood the impossible odds of

21

getting a job, she had joined the tens of millions of the unemployed in the country in being jaded and leaving everything to God and fate. Now, with a job dangled before her eyes and taken away, the volcano had erupted inside her. She opened her mouth to speak, but no sound came out.

She got up and blundered out of there, dazed. The world had started to spin noticeably, and human voices sounded otherworldly and disembodied to her. She couldn't recount what had just happened, nor could she make sense of much thereafter; only much later did the events of much of that day reconstruct themselves in her mind, and even then the recollection had been in bits and pieces. Despair had dulled her senses and kept her twice removed from incidents unfolding wherever she stood, sat, or lay.

While adrift, she caught three buses to find herself at a flat in Proceedings. Her instinct for survival had kicked in and guided her to a place she could quiet her demons. Solitude always eluded her at home, with Big Mama always there and ready for conversation. The flat seemed ideal for her purpose today; after all, she'd had her quiet moments there before. She used her keys to let herself into the vacant flat, relocked the door, and welcomed the deep shadows and stuffy air in the place. She sat on the floor of the living room, kicked off her shoes, and leaned her back against the wall. Perturbed voices continued to ring in her head and sow chaos in her mind. She brought out her notebook, thumbed it absent-mindedly as she gazed into space to bear her torment. This time the coping mechanism failed her. The decibel levels of the distressing sirens in her head suddenly increased so drastically she felt that the roof of her head would blow off any second and that she was at the tipping point of madness.

Her reflex kicked in. She began to take slow lungful of breaths, breathing deeply and heavily. Every breath she took reached the bottom of her stomach. Nothing automatic about the breathing—she breathed methodically and conscientiously the way children new to breathing do. Every breath began to assert itself as a psychic force. Gradually the haunting voices in her head started to drop their decibel levels. As they did so, she became increasingly attuned to the cloistered character of a flat that seemed abandoned to her, to its stillness, to the whiff of antiquity in the air, to the cave-like atmosphere around her. The perturbed voices died out, and her mind stopped spinning. She became tranquil. Time passed; she didn't notice.

Elizabeth must have dozed off when banging on the door of the apartment startled her. Panic seized her—heart thumping like a drum. *Who is that? Who is that? The landlord? The owner? Who?* Few weeks ago, she had gotten the keys of the flat in the general way that most CDKurienes got a place to rent. Landlords in that supercharged rental market required (despite the legal three-month limit) two years' rent in advance, along with a million assorted fees; people who hadn't amassed such wealth scrambled to win the confidential contest to sublet from the rare tenant moving out. If the vigilant landlord discovered the new tenant, both negotiated new terms and life went on.

Elizabeth hadn't really scrambled for the flat. The prior tenant had simply handed her the keys and Elizabeth had clasped them in her palms—both of them dreaming she would soon get a job and move into the flat. Well, she still did not have a job. In her current financial state, she couldn't negotiate the required advance payment; in fact, she had no money even to make monthly payments. Hence had she swallowed hard, gotten up slowly and tiptoed to the door to peer through the peephole. A light-complexioned face with magnified buckteeth filled up her vision. She escaped to the restroom with her shoes and handbag, but remembered her notebook too late.

The man entered the apartment with another set of the keys and pulled a curtain. He gave a perfunctory look to the living room, drifted toward the bedrooms and restrooms, and drifted back. He had seen the notebook. When he got it, he opened it and began to read. Anger that a stranger was reading her "heirloom" emboldened Elizabeth to rush out of her hiding place to confront the young man. "That's mine," she charged.

"What are you doing here?" he asked sternly.

"What are you doing here?" she countered, still encouraged by her anger.

"My father—my former father and I own the place. Now, what are you doing here?"

She simply told him about her plans to sublet the place once she got a job. When she finished, he muttered, "Honesty. A refreshing attribute!" His eyes looked up for the first time to take her in, and she found herself arrested by a gaze that seemed to see through to her deep dark secrets. Feeling uneasy, she fidgeted. "Where do you live now?" he asked.

"I live with my uncle in Irnopi."

"You have a cell number?"

"No."

"Your address?"

She caught on that he wanted to see her again and flared up. "Please give me my notebook!"

He gave it to her and said, "I don't want anyone

surprising me in the middle of the night. Please give me the keys."

She threw them at him with vehemence and ran away from there.

#

At night, Don's shocking news confined Elizabeth to a solitary and haunted spot on the bed. Nothing in the rooms manifested itself fully in her mind; any sensation of the night that she would later recall had drifted into her subconscious mind. Don's accusation still mystified her, still stunned her into only being able to repeat his statement in her mind: *But you made me look like a fool, like an idiot.* She had no clue how not honoring the lunch invitation made him look like an idiot. A little hurt perhaps—he was the type. But disgraced? Were others involved? He did allude to his secretary, and had this been a better time, she would have been racking her brains to puzzle out the point of that allusion. However, she was too defeated and dazed for mental exercise.

Memories of her job odyssey, which she'd strategically pushed to the back of her mind, washed over her. The tramping around, the office ambushes to find executives with the magic wand, the thick desperation in the air that predisposed millions to offering bribes of boatloads of cash or sexual favors for employment and that made executives (aka ogres) greedy for more, the circle after circle of futile job quest—all played out bitterly in her mind. Some time ago, she'd thought that her last spark of hope had died—today she felt certain of that. She lay on the bed sapped and disembodied as the zest for life leaked out of the holes that despair had dug in her soul. She felt like a sack of bones—like a skeleton without animating force or pulse. She zonked out on the bed, her mind lost to depression and to a seemingly permanent darkness with no way out.

The midnight hour had come and gone, yet not once had the blades of the fan stirred in the rooms. Heat in there, high enough to melt hard candy, keyed Elizabeth's sweat. She was awash in it from scalp to waist. Yet she lay still on the soggy bed for a long time without feeling the usual discomfort of soaked bedding. Mind over matter. Something else about the incident drifted into her mind: whatever she might have unwittingly done had cut deeply into Don, for he seemed genuinely depressed about the whole thing too.

At dawn, Elizabeth's despair refused to subside, and she didn't come any closer to knowing her undisclosed offense, why he reacted the way he did, and why he was sad about the entire matter.

Long afterward, her misery dragged on. She shuttered herself from the world. She ate only because she had to. Even her favorite dish of rice and stew tasted bland; so, only a morsel of food reached her stomach each day. She spoke as few words as possible because her tongue felt leaden and strange—like the tongue of someone else speaking through her. She had to bathe. She did—mechanically. She had to breathe. Her sour mood couldn't control her beating heart. Day after day, her despondence continued and she moped around indoors. Big Mama's concern grew. "Go to your friend," she said in an attempt to prod the young one out of the house. "See if you can get clothes to retail." But the trade had run its course—money had dried up for most people she knew. The old woman decided that her rescue mission now warranted invoking an anecdote, a near-tragic story that anyone who knew her had heard.

\#

Sixteen years ago, Big Mama was an eligible bachelorette who had supposedly struck gold twice: a university graduate for a suitor and an employed one at that in the midst of massive joblessness. So what that she hardly knew him and that she was a six-footer and he had to stand on his toes to stretch near to her neck? He promised a charmed life in the awe-inspiring city of CDKuru. Her ego, her parents, her friends, and her relatives all fell for all that glittered. She married him. But on arrival at his single room in the magical city, she found that her short husband had (of all the accursed luck on earth!) the most severe shortage of amenities she'd ever seen.

At the time, she hadn't discovered that he'd padded his suitor's resume outrageously—he had actually flunked out of the university and had carried on as if nothing had happened. So her issue then was her nightmarish existence in a slum that seethed with crowds and brimmed with filth. Her dream—an aggregate of so many people's hopes—had morphed into a waking nightmare.

Every night she rebelled in the bedroom like the supporters of Lysistrata who, by the way, had it easier than Big Mama. They could tell their husbands to stop the war or else no lovemaking! She couldn't tell her husband, "Get rich or else …" So she kept quiet about her frustration but feigned headache each night he came close to her in bed. He did, however, start to bluff of returning to the mistresses he'd left for marriage. The young wife, ignorant then of the mores of CDKuru, believed that a poor man could find a mistress there—actually believed that her new husband was a reformed Casanova on the cusp of relapsing.

Unfortunately, the man came home one day with the

smell and smear of lipstick on his white shirt—a red lipstick smear. Some gossips say she grabbed her pestle and threw it at him, knocking him unconscious; others say (perhaps because of her size) that she physically manhandled her featherweight of a husband. No matter how she did it, in a fit of temper she had laid the man out. Believing for a split-second that she had committed murder, she found herself instantly praying and vowing to God, to Allah, to deities on land and water that she would never again pine for a comfortable life if only they would let the supine man get up and stay alive. And when the man recovered enough to pull out the lipstick from his pocket, she was so relieved she immediately conceived a daughter for him and became at peace with her life in general.

"Elizabeth," Big Mama now said. "Gossips like to tell my story their own way. They like to say that the jealous woman almost killed her husband. It wasn't that I was jealous."

They were sitting in the first room—the old woman on the settee, the young one on the bed. For once, the coffee table between them seemed like a huge gulf to Elizabeth. For once, the dim light in the room seemed like an impenetrable darkness. Grief had quarantined her a million miles away to listen to and watch the old woman. "It was that all my hopes of a better life had crashed. I was depressed—I couldn't leave this room. I would sit here and mope and mope. Every day! I couldn't eat. I should have fainted from a hunger strike that I didn't plan. Every day, my heart hurt so much I thought I would die—like a ball of excruciating pain kept stretching my heart to breaking point. Yet he didn't care. He just didn't care. Something came over me."

She heaved a sigh, shook her head ruefully, and folded her arms over her bosom. "You see, I learned about feeling hurt.

28

I know how it feels when a sad event cuts into you. I've learned all that from experience. I also learned that with time, your wound would heal. Right now it is very raw and your pain is so much you think it is killing you. Time will make you feel better. Now when I look back at that sad situation, I wonder why I felt so much pain then. Now the whole thing seems to me like something that happened to me in a different world, in a bad dream. So just know that your gloom shall come to pass also."

# CHAPTER 3

If Elizabeth would stop being half-dead, she didn't in the next few days. She was the same as she had been the week before and since the incident. Yet the old woman hesitated before her next move. Wisdom had slowed her down—her wisdom about how tragedy stunned, about how unimaginably deep psychic pain could be, about … Pity softened her up, and she couldn't bring swift tough love to Elizabeth in the midst of deep hurt—she simply couldn't just dispatch Elizabeth to her prior routine without giving her time to convalesce. So the old woman waited and waited as Elizabeth continued to dawdle around in the dim room and moon about with no sign of recovery. Finally Big Mama pointed at the door, commanded Elizabeth to go on an outing and vowed, "I will not lose you just like that." Thus was Elizabeth able to step out of the compound one morning around eleven.

Outside, smog fogged up every air space. The sky hung quite low, almost overhead. Heavy haze buried everyone and everything on the streets. The city seemed to have shrunk to a gray cloudy dome. Outside, heat retained its notorious edge. Though the official temperature was eighty-four degrees, numerous conditions nudged the heat index way up—humid air, proliferating warrens of asphalt roads, mountain-high skyscrapers across the coastlines of the ocean and the lagoons, jungle of concrete landscapes and cement buildings, and sooty clouds from jam-packed cars everywhere, from millions of electric generators, and from unregulated factories. Out there, the heat menaced with its unspoken threat to broil CDKurienes slowly.

Elizabeth had taken a few steps on the dirt track when the humid heat drew its first flood of sweat out of her. This was faster than usual, for she hadn't been out there in a long time. She dabbed her forehead and neck with a handkerchief as she continued her exit from the slum, carefully sidestepping scattered potholes and mounds of trash on the track toward the thoroughfare. The whole place reeked. Foul smells from numerous slushy gutters, from rotten garbage in the side gullies, and from untreated feces and larger wastes in the back gully all amalgamated into a stale, decaying stench. Though she felt like fleeing from the stench, she couldn't muster speed or quickness on that terrain—her shoes had bent heels.

She held her breath to allow into her lungs as little of the nauseating air as possible. Otherwise, the full-figured young woman, who was five feet eight, looked poised. She was wearing a cotton shift gown of deep green and burgundy colors, and her hair, braided tiny and packed in a bun at the back of the head, allowed the high cheekbones, dimples, enormous eyes, and luscious lips to stand out even while meshing into a chocolate face that was serene and heart-shaped.

When she reached W Avenue, she dithered—she actually had no destination in mind. Automobiles clanged and shrieked on the thoroughfare. Horns blared continuously. Pedestrians hurried along. The overhead and ground lanes, which made the thoroughfare more of a highway than an avenue, bustled with perpetual motion. Elizabeth couldn't loiter there anymore. She had to find somewhere to visit.

One place entered her mind, but she rejected it off-hand. She couldn't return to the flat in Proceedings—that young man must have moved in and she no longer had the keys. Her legs started to move, to carry her south toward Niatsoc Bus Stop. She got there and entered a bus. In about an hour, she had gotten near a destination she'd chosen subconsciously. She was within walking distance of the glass towers of National Natural Resources Corporation in V Island.

She trudged along the shortest path to the corporation, through the concrete parking lot where cars gleamed and glinted and some chauffeurs clustered around in a few quasi-shaded spots to make small talk. She had to see Don and nothing—not the pool of sweat in her armpits, not the right toe that rubbed on the inside of the shoe, not whatever lay at the bottom of this trip—could stop her now. She kept her pace toward the main entrance of the corporation. She paused for initial scrutiny by the coterie of guards at the gate, paused again for another scrutiny by a mixed group of guards and semi-reception staff at another station, and then regained her determined pace into the atrium.

The atrium, wide W-shaped and high as a two-story, led to three towers, two of which faced each other, while the third, the executive tower, sprawled out the entire rear. Each tower had seven floors. Her destination was the fourth floor of the executive tower. She hesitated. In the cool comfort of the atrium, with small crowds dashing to elevators, she stood still. Elizabeth was having an attack of the nerves. *Why have I returned here? Why? He did say that … I really shouldn't be here.* But she started to move again when she remembered Don's look during the debacle. He had looked defeated! And by the time the elevator clicked off on the fourth floor, her mind had settled on why she'd come here. *I have to know why he looked like that and why he accused me of making him look like a fool. Look like a fool! Look like a fool to whom? What did I do or say to cause that?* Her steps would have become fast and furious on the floor at this time, for the burning questions in her mind had just put her in a fiery mood; however, she had to be careful with her unbalanced shoes. So she plodded into Don's reception room.

The room was large, rectangular, and milk-colored. It had about fifteen guest seats—black mid-back box seats with mahogany legs—along the four walls. Four office chairs behind four tables flanked both sides of the door to the inner office. Guests sat on almost all the seats to wait for their admission into the sanctum. One person chose to stand: a character clad in an ample purple robe of lace material—a short charcoal-hued man who was thickset and round as Buddha. He hovered around the largest of the office tables, an imposing L-shaped mahogany desk bearing two computers of different generations, a telephone, a pad of guest questionnaires, and the plaque *Madam Agnes, Executive Secretary.*

The heralded madam—short, chubby, and bewigged— sat behind the table in an executive seat of brown leather with nail head trim accents. She sat high on it as if on a stool. In her fifties, the woman had natural dark-brown skin and small frosty eyes that seemed to censure the world from the depths of an over-fed face. She was wearing a wig and a white silk blouse, a round-neck with ruffled cuffs, over black skirt. And it must be noted that she wore the wig with carnival flair. The hair was jet-black, extraordinarily high, and too textured even for a young woman, let alone a near-retiree. "Welcome, my daughter," she greeted Elizabeth with a grin wide to the ears.

This woman was not Elizabeth's long dead mother suddenly reincarnated; the woman was Don's maternal relative and his father's confidant. She'd used the term "my daughter" as endearment. She held on to her grin—the face now inflated like a soccer ball and the narrow eyes more like slits—as she fawned over Elizabeth, got an employee to vacate his seat for her so she could sit an arms-length away, and then told the quarry over and over that her presence in that office had been long overdue. Elizabeth did not know what to make of these, but she forced herself to keep smiling and nodding ever so slightly to the secretary's amiable talk. Suddenly the woman's face darkened and she burst out, "Worthless girls! The harlots just want Don's money."

Elizabeth scanned the room for the "worthless girls." Instead, she found something odd—a new phenomenon there. Every one of the special guests who had never before spent a second in the reception room had planted his or her ample, skinny, or flat buttocks on a seat. Each of them used to call Don on the cell phone from downstairs to have him alert the secretary to wave the person in to the inner office as soon as he or she appeared in the reception room. Elizabeth had once asked Don why those people flouted the protocol for getting into his inner office; he had said he would get her a cell phone so she could do the same. She had refused.

A few people sauntered into the office and to the madam's table to write their names and purpose of visit on a form before retreating to a corner to stand now that guest seats had filled up. Pulling her gaze briefly from Elizabeth, the woman warned the new arrivals with authority, "He won't see many people today." Madam Agnes sounded very much in charge now, a new generalissimo. *Perhaps,* thought Elizabeth, *the woman had something to do with Don's explosion last time ...*

*Didn't he allude to her?*

Elizabeth scanned the room again. The glazed eyes and yawning mouths of most guests told her they had waited too long. No one made small talk or tried to chat. No one texted or made calls either. The only life in the room came from the rotund man and three young women in a silent rivalry. First, the man compelled attention by blocking the direct path to the secretary's table. Then, he adjusted his ample robe ceaselessly so that his watch could enjoy the spotlight as well. He would pull the left voluminous open sleeve that reached a foot beyond his fingers up to the shoulder; the sleeve would refuse to stay put and would roll down his arm to shroud the watch. Yet the right hand continued to work on and on. Elizabeth named him Sisyphus.

Beyond him, the three women conducted their cold war. One glared across the room at a rival, but the rival carried on with an aloofness fit for a queen, hanging her head in the sky and pointedly looking away from the orbit of that other woman to underscore the woman's status as a nonentity. The royal attitude suggested who got more of Don's attention. As for the third woman, she had come brash and ready in a state of undress. Her mini gear, with spaghetti strings, fastened itself tight enough to her voluptuous physique to scandalize conventional minds, as should her bold and dramatic make-up of a cake face, hot-pink lips, arching tar-black eyebrows, purple eye shadow, and long eyelashes with heavy coats of Mascara. That she was overdone, like a geisha, and chomping away on her gum announced her buccaneering intent and added to the tension in the triangle.

Elizabeth, captured by the silent drama, wondered with an intensity that scowled her face why Don could have devoted an entire week to her with all these going on around him.

"Don't worry about anything," cajoled Madam Agnes, who must have misread the scowl as a sign of frustration for the delay in seeing Don.

Those mollifying words set off a frenzy of responses among guests who could decipher preferential treatment and access in an office. Sisyphus responded first. He initially moved his bulky frame right to the front of the secretary's table, then stepped closer. Three others joined him. They had crowded the secretary's table to mount a subtle campaign against what was about to happen and to affirm without alienating Madam Agnes that they had arrived here before the favored girl, duly filled out the form to see Don, and intended to see him before she did.

"I've waited long enough," one said to the executive secretary.

"When am I seeing him?" said another.

"Is he even going to see anyone today?"

"I have to see him," Sisyphus bellowed as if the negative overtone of the last question was a personal affront to him. He then brought his left wrist to a vantage point for every nearby eye (especially madam's) to see his watch, which had a gilded symbol of a crown and a champagne dial. He made a show of checking time on it, though the large office clock loomed directly in his line of vision, and muttered aloud with a scowl, "Twelve thirty-one! Rolex is never wrong." Then he said to the secretary, "You know it's MD that I want 'The Don' to help me with. It's very important." Translation: His deal was too big for Don; only the managing director could handle it.

Madam Agnes wasn't impressed. She said in a monotone to the man and to all who'd reminded her of their mission, "He's still busy." Then she pressed the pneumatic control of her chair to lower her bulk. When her feet touched the floor, she heaved herself up from the seat, trudged on high heels to the door of the inner office, rapped on it and vanished inside. A minute later, she poked her head out, beckoned Elizabeth to the door, ushered her into the office and took herself out, closing the door softly to a few agitated voices.

Elizabeth entered the office and saw the joy in Don's narrow eyes as he came towards her for a hug of welcome. At close range, she saw yet again that his distinctive features were his lanky stature, his youthful face, and a big mashed-in nose that wasn't jarring to look at on that face. You had to catch the nose in isolation to say to yourself, "Hmm, that nose." He was wearing pinstripe suit in his usual slim-fit style, a style she'd once and still considered too indexed to a specific weight—if he gained just two and a half pounds, he would find squeezing into his clothes impossible. A six-footer, he had to bend to hug her.

For a moment after hugging, his smile waned and his face sagged in disappointment. "What happened?" he asked but regretted asking when she didn't answer. "Never mind."

He held her hand, and she let him. They enjoyed these warm moments standing in the middle of the spacious office. Then, with an encouraging smile, he steered her to one of the guest seats, before moving to his chair.

What a difference the prodigal friend's unexpected return had made. Last time, his animosity filled this office; today, she is an egg to be carried delicately!

From his chair, Don leaned across the table toward Elizabeth. "I tried to find you," he said in a weary voice as his eyes briefly hooded with sadness. "But I didn't know where to find you. You have no cell. Your application has a post office number."

His conduct baffled her again. *Why that unmistakable sad face again? What did he lose in the incident? Maybe he lost a little dignity—maybe! I lost something priceless. A job is no ego-tripping. A job is proof of accomplishment—tangible proof! What exactly did he lose in that incident that gives him this puppy face?* She heard herself asking in a tiny voice, "What happened last time?"

Silence. She would have suspected that he didn't hear her had his wounded look not returned. She hushed, too. The situation had become delicate. Apparently, he did not want a confrontation. Elizabeth thought it would be unfair to press him for the answer in his moment of truce. So she simply waited for an opportune time. The low hum of the air conditioner became audible.

Eventually he reached for his cell, punched in his password, and held the device in his palm, ready to type. He asked softly and slowly for her address, concluding he didn't want a repeat of what happened last time. When she said she had no address, he tried to humor her. "You do not live under the bridge," he said lightly. "Come on, Elizabeth, tell me where you live."

"Seriously, my house has no address."

"I am not an idiot, you know," he said with a sudden trace of anger. "I can take a hint."

"There's no hint there," she exclaimed. "My uncle's house has no address!"

"Come on, every house in CDKuru has an address." But doubt had crept into his voice.

"Not in Irnopi where I live."

It's doubtful he'd heard the name before, but the fervor in her tone got him. He studied her face in utter silence for a few seconds. Then he wanted to know how visitors found their hosts there.

"Drive one mile from Niatsoc Bus Stop," she began, "and turn right on a dirt track by the side of a walled-in three-story building, turn left at the junction, ask anyone you meet for—"

"This is chancy," Don interjected, looking somewhat befuddled.

"No," she said in an attempt to continue.

"Don't worry," he said. "I'll drive you home today."

Elizabeth fell into reflective silence. Eventually she asked firmly and loudly, "What happened last time, Don?"

"You see," he began and then paused a long time to frame his thoughts diplomatically. "Don't worry about the past; the future is bright. My motto is 'forgive and forget.' That's me."

Although Elizabeth had the fleeting concern that she couldn't tell from Don's phrasing who was forgiving whom (was he forgiving her or was he asking to be forgiven?), she believed in forgetting. Forgetting, she would say, kept the bad memory away and allowed somebody to have some sort of peace of mind about a past that the person's infinite regrets could not change now. She nodded her assent.

Don continued, "All is not lost. Madam Agnes will talk to my dad to get the thing done."

In gratitude, she almost flew out of her seat into Don's arms. The lump of grievance that had grown in her heart from his action last time had started to melt away. Her need to

40

understand what happened or didn't happen last time no longer pressed her. Until a few moments ago, she'd come to believe she came here to get an explanation for his puzzling conduct during her last visit; now, on hearing all was not lost, her need for an explanation ebbed. She would still like to know, but she wouldn't go too far afield for answers now.

She became light-hearted and could entertain a joke. *All is not lost, he had said. I hope he hadn't used that phrase in the right context. Or is he now Satan after God had vanquished him in Paradise Lost? "What though the field be lost? All is not lost ...*" Her joke made her smile to herself.

However, he noticed the smile. "What's funny?"

"It's not important. Idle stuff."

"I like idle stuff. Tell me."

"Do you remember Paradise Lost?"

"That sounds important. That's no fun. Let's not worry about that."

Well, Don and Elizabeth had just acted alike in one respect: they wanted to know, but then didn't want to know. He'd said he wanted to know why she smiled, but when the answer seemed to be growing complicated he opted out. She herself had felt for some time that she wanted to know why Don aggrieved her last time, but now, face to face with him, she really didn't need to know. Why had an issue that had convulsed her for weeks suddenly generated tepid interest in her? Why? Why had the burning questions of a few minutes ago become academic? Why?

The blunt answer was that out of habit she had automatically found a way to escape a negative emotion. Earlier today, when her legs turned toward the bus stop and trudged

41

onward to Don's office, she had done so for at least two reasons. She had done so in small part to understand what happened there last time. She had done so in large part to satisfy her latent wish to get back the job that Don had told her she'd lost weeks ago. However, she couldn't acknowledge the wish to herself because of the shame of admitting to herself that she was crawling back to a man who had dismissed her. So she had secreted that wish away until a few minutes ago.

CHAPTER 4

For now, to say that Elizabeth had become soft as marshmallows would be an understatement. Now Don could say whatever he wanted to say about that day, and she would listen without the slightest rise in blood pressure. "I made a mistake when my dad went to Miami and LA," he began. "They rushed him to the doctor when he came back. I had to do something to get his blood pressure down. So Madam Agnes packaged something for me. I have to look busy—keep my 'bad friends' away from the office, 'look responsible.' Only one cell stays on in the office—for mom and dad. Now people are not coming into my office willy-nilly. You see, I'm trying my best." He paused, rolled his shoulders a few times, and looked away.

She stared at him. He had used the word "people" euphemistically. *Why don't you say "girls"? Or be like Madam Agnes and call them "worthless girls."* She now had a general sense of the show Don and Madam Agnes were putting up for his father. Don had to act as if he'd outgrown being a ladies' man, as if he'd entered the settling down phase of his life. *Oh no! Better not be that!* She was suddenly suspicious of having a major part in the scheme.

He continued, "All that week, I had to make sure dad saw me having lunch at the senior staff canteen. He had to see me there alone or with you any day you came."

"Why me?"

"Well … well … not every girl can look like someone's steady girlfriend," he said with a laugh. "Besides, Madam Agnes said that you are the only girl I know who can convince my dad that I have become serious in life."

"Why would she say that?"

"She said something like you don't come here to take my money and act almighty. But I know one thing for sure: dad loves education. And you are too much—a master's and more in accountancy for a pretty girl."

*Lizzy, please don't worry about his mild sexism now. Let him know later that studying accounting does not require excessive testosterone. Learning is not weight lifting. Later, please, later.* She asked, "Why didn't you tell me of the plan that day?"

"I know you would have refused—"

"No matter what, you should have told me."

"I just wanted you to help me—didn't want to make too much noise about it. I waited all week, you know."

"I didn't say I would make it," she said evenly.

"You said, 'Let's see,'" he tried to counter.

"Then why think I'd come?"

Don was flustered. A shallow thinker, he couldn't make his case for expecting her, which made him seem impulsive or even insane. Of course, he hadn't heard a voice say that Elizabeth would make the lunch date and that was that. He had a basis for his belief. Had he plumbed his mind, he would have noted that when she came out with her ambiguous response to the lunch invitation—her "Let's see"—she'd sent two signals. One could be she was being coy and would show up; another could be, as her position became clear in hindsight, she won't come. In any case, the hair-splitting would have been avoided had she simply said she couldn't make it. Eventually Don found his voice. "I did believe you would come."

Something was still missing from his account—the place

44

of her job issue in the whole story. She asked and he tried to supply that detail. "Madam Agnes had told me to let you know that if you had come that week, you would have gone home with a job."

*That's not really how you said it. But why bother? You won't understand the difference between what you said that day and what you just said. Besides, the past is the past. We have to avoid what we can of a past that caused us or still causes us pain.* Indeed, he told her something essentially different on that occasion. He had morphed a message intended to get Elizabeth in line into something else. He had added his two cents' worth then and veered off message. He'd been so thick with pent-up fury that he'd spoken in such hopeless, final, irreconcilable terms that he had foreclosed any chances of her getting the job back. "Sorry I just can't help you anymore," he had declared. Had she taken those words to heart and not let her desperation bring her back here, then what? His type just didn't make good accomplices.

#

At times, a single incident between two people behind closed doors refuses to be contained therein. Emotions, thoughts and actions born of that incident carry past the orbit of the two involved to the heart and mind of someone else. At this point, the genie is out of the bottle; at this point, selective amnesia about the incident might as well be a delusional exercise. And so even if Don and Elizabeth forgot about that disastrous day completely—forgot it to the last detail—they still couldn't hypnotize everyone else who knew of it directly or indirectly to lose that memory, nor could they wipe out the aftermath of that particular incident. In short, even if Don's father redeemed his son and got Elizabeth the job, the matter wouldn't tidily die and be forgotten—for it had already set other things in motion.

One such thing was the dogged search for Elizabeth by the man she had encountered briefly after drifting out of Don's office that ignominious day. She would learn of that development around ten o'clock one morning when a knock brought her to the door to ask, "Who is it?"

"May I come in?" the voice answered.

Elizabeth's hand, outstretched and ready to pull the curtain, froze. She had identified the person at her door—the man she had encountered in the vacant Proceedings flat on that fateful day and had refused his request for her contact information. Yes, a blur of that encounter entered her mind occasionally, but she hadn't imagined she would ever see him again—hence her shock.

When she didn't speak or pull the curtain, the man asked again, "May I come in?"

She remained stunned. Questions began popping up in her mind. *How did he find me? Why did he come? Does he think we have unresolved issues about the flat?* ... Though she still couldn't speak, her hand pulled the curtain.

He entered the room. She flicked the switch on to take advantage of the rare supply of electricity. The ceiling fan creaked out a gentle breeze. Sunlight nibbling at the curtain and at the window combined with light from the bulb inside to make the room bright enough to reveal the visitor clearly. Light-skinned, he was lean, in the late twenties and about five feet nine. He had an oval face under a full head of naturally curly hair, narrow monolid eyes with arresting gaze, and barely noticeable gap teeth. He wore a beige polo shirt, loose khaki pants and black walking shoes. Looking comfortable and casually chic in that hot weather, he had a calm presence.

She relaxed. The questions in her mind vanished—except one. *How was he able to find me?* Indeed, how was he able to find her in CDKuru? This was a city of about twenty million with records for only thousands. Here, neighborhoods existed that did not make it into the city map. Citizens had no identification numbers or a single form of citywide identification. Moreover, majority of residents did not have their names recorded anywhere for whatever reason (for medical treatment, driver's license, taxation) since penury consigned them to an underground existence of sorts. Therefore, to find her on the strength of the name of her neighborhood and her looks, which he had seen just once, was indeed remarkable.

"How did you find me?" she wondered aloud after he sat down.

"Irnopi has at least one characteristic of a small town," he said. "Everybody knows everybody."

"They don't know my—you don't even know my name."

"No names needed—just appearances."

"I look like a million girls here."

"You still have certain peculiarities."

"Like what?"

He said jovially, "Like making things difficult for me."

She laughed, and then said, "You appeared from nowhere that day. Besides, I was having a terrible day."

"What about?"

She told him.

"Your honesty is refreshing," he said when she finished.

47

"It calls for a toast."

She thought he was being sarcastic and told him so.

"I am serious," he said. "I was beginning to lose faith in humanity." He dipped his hand into his pocket, brought out some money, and told her to buy two bottles of whatever beverage she drank.

She began to laugh. People didn't toast such a thing. They toasted love, happiness, success, long life; no one but this young man drank to honesty. After the laughter she said, "Your idea is odd but sensible, especially in this place where dishonest men and women have destroyed everything. … Thanks. But wrong time and wrong place for the toast." She had recognized that for her to laugh and drink with a stranger that early in the morning too would not look good for Big Mama to see.

"All right," he said as he pocketed the money.

"Now, what about my other peculiarities?"

"Well, the dimples, the dressing to hide your shape, the reserved look—"

"You told them, 'the reserved look'?"

"No," he said. "I told them, 'She keeps to herself and doesn't stay outside to chat with neighbors."

She asked in awe, "One quick look at me that day and you got all that?"

"Certain things are not that mysterious," he said. "If you had adjusted to life here, you would not have been rushing to leave."

"You mean my foolish rush—"

"Yes," he said coolly, "your foolish rush to fool around with getting a flat."

"Are you always this way with people?"

"Honesty is the best policy."

"I hope honesty is not your obsession."

"You might call it my pursuit."

She sighed and said, "I hope you've not wasted your time and initiative looking for me."

"Nothing wasted," he said. "Nothing is ever wasted in that journey inward."

"Are you a philosopher or a psychologist?"

"Neither but both," he offered enigmatically.

"Are you a detective or a journalist?"

"Neither but both," he said again.

"Stop being mysterious and please give me a straight answer," she said in a jocular tone.

"You will get the answers you really need when you stop asking leading questions," he responded with a smile.

Chuckling, Elizabeth said, "All right, mystery man who knows all about me."

Then he spoke in earnest, "You know the place. Come for a visit."

"You come to Suhccab instead. Friday night. Ask for the Don's table."

"The Don's table," he repeated dubiously. "I don't want to be in the middle of anything."

"You won't be. Don't worry."

"All right."

"By the way," she said as she offered her hand, "my name is Elizabeth Kōp."

He shook her hand and simply introduced himself as Gideon.

Later, long after he exited the room, his initial doubt

about joining her at Don's table infected her. Questions besieged her. *Have I made an impulsive mistake? Have I? Should I go to his apartment to cancel the invitation? Or am I being gullible for worrying about this just because of his initial doubts?*

#

An array of bulbs jutting from the ceiling and upper walls flooded Suhccab with lights in a dramatic interplay as a rainbow of motion, strobe, and disco lights dimmed, flared, and circled the smoky atmosphere. All was visible, though tinged orange and continually surreal with the slow magic of the lights. Music pulsated. And those who came to showcase their dance moves strutted as the lights replicated their moves, animated them at a hyperactive clip, and whirled their images into a heady choreographed spectacle. Others, too, did what they'd come to do: They preened or tried to impress, mingled with a select crowd, gawked …

Suhccab was a colossal tri-level of about four-story high, elliptical and grandiose. Even so, furniture and design elements made the club feel cozy and intimate. Its raised dance floor—a three-quarter thrust stage with underfloor lights and transparent columns—sloped a few steps onto the floor that had cross-sections of egg seats for the general public on both sides of a semi-circular aisle. Two stairwells descended onto the floor from the place to be: the mezzanine lounge, where some celebrities carried on like peacocks. This lounge, subdivided into three, advertised its exclusive status with ornate murals of sea nymphs and satyrs on three walls and with a Mahogany balustrade with crisscross wood ornaments. Sofas of various body parts (heart, hand, lips) and deep egg seats further distinguished the section.

The lounge's distinguished look and elevation alone

would have instinctively drawn eyeballs up there anyway. Yet the main reason people gawked at that reserved section was sheer human vanity. They gawked because by some magical osmosis by being in a general area with a celebrity the star-struck became a minor celebrity. So they obsessed to identify celebrities in attendance that night so as to preen afterwards about whom they saw at Suhccab.

Though Don was no celebrity—at least not yet or at least not in the usual way—he had a table in the lounge. He merited that table largely through his prodigious spending at the club. He was at his table with his entourage: Bode Ojjug, his two female companions, Gideon, and Elizabeth. All of them shared two sofas and two egg seats in a V-shaped arrangement that created an intimate space around their table. Don sat with Elizabeth on the heart-shaped sofa, Bode with his mistress on the hand-shaped sofa, the other girl and Gideon on the egg seats. Tonight Elizabeth's natural grace beguiled more than ever. She'd let her long micro-braided hair, packed from the face, to fall to her back and allowed her full lips a touch of burgundy lipstick. She wore a decent cotton shift dress that was also her size, and her shape did wonders to the light brown dress that (Holy of Holies!) matched the color of Gideon's pants.

The DJ turned down his music and announced, "The Don is in the house." Don lifted his right hand slowly in a show of grudging acknowledgment of the introduction—though he assiduously courted the echo of his name in that club by buying the DJ drinks. He wore a well-tailored lime Mandarin suit of linen material. Someone said to him, "Nice Suit." Another interjected, "Hundred per cent lino." Don beamed. CDKurienes recognized quality when they saw it. Italian linen recognized just like that! "Puro lino," he added with aplomb.

But his self-confidence faltered and he fidgeted when he found himself in the radar of Gideon's cool stare. Gideon, himself, wore a loose tunic with front pockets, baggy pants, and matching sandals. He sat quite at ease with himself, just watching the other man and the world in a rather disinterested way. Then the rivalry started. Don instantly draped his arm quite close to Elizabeth's shoulders without touching her. He'd laid his claim; in his own way, he was saying to the good guest, "She is my woman." He wasn't dissuaded that the "she" in question sat uptight, fighting the urge to push him away.

To strengthen his position, Don began to show off that he belonged to an elite circle and relapsed into ostentatious spending when the waitress came to get orders from his table. He kept her for minutes detailing the VIPs whose tab he would pick up tonight: Prof So-and-So, Doctor So-and-So, Engineer So-and-So, Architect So-and-So, Director So-and-So. He'd retrieved his arm from Elizabeth's back to point them out, though the men needed no introduction. "Tell them it's the Don's night." When they waved acknowledgement later, he went on a tour of their tables for vigorous handshakes, small talk, and shared smiles.

His crass use of titles aside, Don had recognized only the educated. In fact, his insecurities surfaced only amid educated people. He hadn't met the academic expectations of an elite school-educated father, and Don tried too hard to befriend those who would have made his old man proud. Take Elizabeth. When he first met her, he didn't pay her much attention for weeks until he read her resume and became attentive as a hawk. With Gideon, too, things could have been different had it been that after introductions—after Elizabeth had pried out his status as junior faculty member on sabbatical and gushed about her father's fond memory of his short-lived faculty life—he had seemed nebbish and lost in the ways of the world. Don would have been full of cheer and without concern. But the other man had looked more and more urbane and unique, looking more like Don Juan than Don Quixote. Thus had Don enlisted the good names of those VIPs and let it be known also that he had money to burn.

Elizabeth sat stiff, her thoughts burning with objections to Don's display. *It is fine to name-drop and show you have money. But please God don't let this continue. Please God put it in his mind that there's something called "wretched excess." It doesn't look good on anybody—not on him and not on me! Worse, he's doing all this because of jealousy for somebody I do not have anything with.*

Well, God failed to intercede on Elizabeth's behalf and Don's greetings remained too boisterous for a sober man. No, he hadn't imbibed anything yet—except, of course, the subliminal threat from the man at the other end. The flush of embarrassment spread like a colony of ants on her face. She got irritated. *I wish he would just sit, wave to the men, and hail them as he had always done in the past.* Her irritation grew when his arm, which sought to mark her off as part of his territory, grazed her shoulder, and instinct almost made her slide down her seat.

The uniformed waitress helped tone down Don's act. When she came back to their table with her tray and her tablet for drink orders, she planted herself in Don's line of vision. Now, despite Don's insecurities or because of them, he had an engaging tongue for small talk. He smiled at the lean young woman, addressed her by name, and made a joke about shots of brandy not created equal by the bartender. "Some are shots," he said, laughing. "Others are shorter." He'd gotten his friends and the waitress laughing.

"Don't worry, Mr. Don," the waitress said after her mirth. "Nobody will short your drinks."

As he laid wads of money on her tray, he told her, "You know I know that. Just teasing. Get something for yourself and the DJ."

"Thank you, sir."

The previously offending arm had come off Elizabeth's back, and Don had cut his charade to order the drinks. "Two shots of Remy [Remy Martin] for everyone on this table," he said, before adding with a nod in Elizabeth's direction, "mortuary-cold malt for the lady here."

Bode and his companions chuckled. The man, about fifty-five years old and five feet seven inches tall, was a portly dark figure with square face and hair of pure gray. He wore round prescription glasses under his heavy eyebrows and looked dignified in his burgundy French suit, though he was a rascal. He'd been friends since childhood with Don's father, who liked to describe Bode humorously as "a late bloomer" for doing now all he could have done in his bachelor days, and that friendship occasionally worked against Don. His father usually knew more about the son's social life (especially the womanizing and the spending) than the son would have liked. Now Bode Ojjug and his two companions in their early twenties were amused as usual that Elizabeth preferred soft drinks.

"Waitress," Gideon called. "Large Stout."

# CHAPTER 5

Elizabeth heard something troubling in Gideon's tone. A matter-of-fact tone, it conveyed his retreat from the group more eloquently than words to that effect. Apparently, the man wanted to remain himself in the midst of her party—he wanted to socialize with the people on her table on his own terms. Her hope for lively conversation when Don went dancing began to dissipate, and she sighed in utter disappointment.

For a second, Don looked stunned. Then he threw a sharp look at Elizabeth; other eyes around the table assailed her too. You would have thought she'd set two men up to start a world war. Helen of Troy didn't get more accusing looks. Elizabeth frowned. *One, Gideon is not my lover or whatever. Two, other girls usually join the party at Don's table when I'm there. Three, if he can invite other girls to the table, why can't I invite a boy? Four, I've picked up that Don brings me here because he's a man scheming out of his relationship with his fading flame, his former queen. Five, all of you giving me the evil eye here are well aware of at least most of the above.* Her frown deepened as she stared right back at him and at those other accusing eyes.

"Everyone on my table gets at least double service," Don said casually to the waitress. "Get him two Stout."

"I am asking for one," Gideon said quietly to the waitress, who still eyed Don.

For the first time, Don challenged the other man directly, "You can handle two bottles—can't you?"

Gideon ignored the challenge and kept his eyes on the

waitress. Elizabeth realized she had misjudged both men. She didn't know Don would be so proprietary, nor did she know Gideon was so individualistic he wouldn't humor Don for the sake of peace. *Now, what am I to do? Don is already in mid-stride. Perhaps, Gideon would accept the two bottles of Stout from the waitress and just drink one.* She watched him and recognized his cool, steady manner of shrouding out the world while penetrating it with a keen gaze. *He has the same sort of poise my father had*, she realized with a start—this Gideon, who was telling the befuddled waitress, "One Stout. Please, a separate bill."

"I'm a poor man, but I can buy you a drink," Don protested.

The happy-go-lucky trio laughed again. "Poor indeed!" Bode said.

"Change of order," Don intoned. "Make it four bottles of Remy for this table and stand by."

"Yes, four bottles of Remy," said Bode. "Spoken like a church-rat."

That elicited a round of laughter. Bode's main sugar baby—a light-skinned and dainty petite with doll-like face, puppy eyes and short spiky hair—turned with a sly, knowing smile to Elizabeth to press home an old point made as soon as both had become acquainted at the club. The small woman had been quite friendly and free with the unsolicited advice that Elizabeth had better seize her opportunity for marriage now. "Stop this business of 'We are just friends,'" she had told Elizabeth after touting Don as a nice and generous gentleman. "You are lucky. You can snatch him now that his parents want him to settle down. Look, he has the means to take care of anything for you—anything! He will not only give you the highlife—your relatives won't have to worry about much. We're talking about Don here!"

Elizabeth fervently believed then, months ago, that the pitch was all wrong. One, you don't pitch marriage to a girl who is barely tiptoeing in an affair, to somebody who has fears of flashbacks of gushing blood whenever her thoughts close in on love, marriage or any such pairings meant to endure. *"Till death do us part!" so vow Christian couples. The trouble is when death parts them and one spouse is alive, young, and too torn to comprehend or bear the loss.* Two, Petite was the most invalid spokesperson for marriage. Mistress of a married man, she'd roped him into their affair so much that Elizabeth imagined with horror his wife's habitual loneliness at night in a sprawling plush home, while the husband had himself tied to another woman to gallivant around town, country and universe. Even now, Petite's complicit smile reached Elizabeth as if it came from rotting teeth and stale breath—the smile made Elizabeth's stomach a little queasy.

The drinks arrived. Four standard bottles of fine Champagne Cognac on Don's table for six people announced an open invitation to people around there. Yes, the elite freeloaded too. They continually drifted to the table to pour themselves drinks, chat with Don, and loiter. They drained the four bottles before the six people on the table got their space back. Four of them swayed off immediately toward the dance floor, leaving Gideon and Elizabeth at the table. An uncomfortable silence attended them for a minute.

"Excuse me," Elizabeth muttered as she got up. Then she huddled to the staircase and descended, hand on the rail for support. She had hardly straightened up on the gangway when she saw the mournful profile of Don's former queen. Now grieving out of his life but still trying to prick his conscience, the girl sat hunched in her now customary posture and seat, lonely and downcast and doomed in the spotlight near the bottom of the stairs, her palm propping up her slumped head. Her swift and severe degradation from the haughty well-groomed girl in Don's office to this apparition with an air of loss startled Elizabeth again. She turned mushy inside with pity and wished she could supply the poor girl the ammunition to fight on. *Don't believe the hype. Don and I are not serious. Fight on, sister ... I can't tell her—I might as well kiss the job goodbye.* The girl saw Elizabeth and awoke from the stupor of her grief. Hatred was her stimulant. She jerked her head up, sat up, and had her eyes direct two beams of pure venom at Elizabeth. If evil eyes could kill, these would have kneed Elizabeth over on the spot and stopped her beating heart then and forever.

But they didn't. Instead, the look incensed Elizabeth whose thought of the other girl became *What a stupid girl!* The girl wasn't done, however. She hissed to Elizabeth's hearing, "May the arranged bride die slowly!"

Elizabeth ignored the curse and pressed on to the restroom. After using the restroom, she loitered, trying to kill time. Suddenly she became agitated in front of the wall-to-wall mirror when Don's spurned lady sprang into Elizabeth's thoughts. *What a stupid girl! What a useless girl! If she had not been a mercenary, would I be here with him? Would I be roped into all this? Wasn't she one of Madam Agnes's "worthless girls"? She must be the main one. See how she was carrying on that day in his office. Yes, yes, what did Madam Agnes tell Don*

58

*about those girls? "They come there to take his money and act almighty." ... Now, however, all that money is going to dry up, the day of reckoning is upon her, and she can't act almighty anymore. Now, we know she has a terror inside too, because she is showing it.*

At this point, Elizabeth backed away from the direction her critique was heading, for it was inching toward her own terror—she veered from it and targeted some more of her acrimony at the other girl. Eventually she got tired of that and returned to her seat, where she pretended to be absorbed in the action on the dance floor though she continued to glance furtively at Gideon. He just sat back in his own space and occupied it with a remarkable air of solitude, gazing out of there at the world. She began to stare at him until he drank from his bottle. She suspected that his internal radar had picked up her stare. Yet he didn't stare back in mild rebuke, humor her with a smile, or make any eye contact that she could respond to. No. He had just carefully lifted the large dark bottle, sipped his Stout, and set the bottle down. She hoped he would go home. At issue here wasn't so much what he had done; it was what he hadn't done. He hadn't overlooked crass and inane behavior; he hadn't allowed himself to just go with the flow so that he could make the most of the company here.

Her stare at him was hardening when Bode returned with the petite one right at his heels.

"Bode," said Elizabeth. "What's the time?"

"Ten twenty-something," he answered after looking at his watch. "It's too early even for you. So stop worrying about time."

Elizabeth usually left around midnight. But her Cold

War with Gideon made the next one hour-plus stretch too far into the future. When Bode and Petite left to dance, time seemed to halt. Gideon turned to watch her without comment.

"I've had better times here," she began.

He didn't let her finish. "This is a place to drink, dance, or show off; not a place to shy away from the arms of a boyfriend."

"Look around," she countered in anger. "I'm not the only one not dancing up here. People come here to lounge, too. Besides, the 'arms' business is not your business." Her anger had to do with many things, especially his uncanny recognition of her discomfort with Don's arm and the ease with which he'd read her private thoughts, whereas she'd had to dig out information about him. She challenged him, "Go home if you can't be social."

He retorted that he would have already gone home if it hadn't taken him so much time to work himself up for this outing.

"A misanthrope?"

"No. Someone who follows his better judgment."

"Why did you come here then?"

"Why did you want me to come here?"

"Look," she said slowly. "When you asked me to visit you, I should have just declined. No need telling you to come here. But you had taken so much trouble to find me. I got carried away. Now I know I made a mistake."

"No mistake at all. You were crying out for help."

She snorted out a laugh and asked, "For help from you?"

"Certainly not from any of these people," he said as he waved in the direction his subjects had been sitting.

"What do you know about them?"

"I know they are all fakes."

"Fakes?"

"Yes, fakes. I spent my entire life with a fake. I can now tell a fake from miles away."

"Tell me how they are fakes."

"Take the one who thinks she's a model. See how she's latching on to a married, old geezer. You think that's love? Even you know she is a fraud."

"Go on."

"Now, the old man. He wants to remain young. So he needs them young. A vampire, he needs young blood to keep his delusions alive. Should I go on?"

"Why not?"

"Your friend. He has such inferiority complex he doesn't even know who he is."

"You had judged him even before he did anything," she accused him.

"No, I didn't. He was already performing before I sat down. Should I continue?"

"Why not. What about me?"

"You?"

"Yes, me."

"You are not one of them yet," he said. "But you will be if you don't take care of your issue."

"I have no issue."

"If you had no issue, you won't be running around with these fakes—"

"Enough about fakes!"

"Your friend is the one helping with the job, right?"

"Don't ask me—you know all there is to know on earth."

"From what you told me, from just keeping my eyes open and observant, I can deduce. That's the gift of education."

"Thanks for that information."

"Apparently, you are waiting for your friend to deliver what he obviously can't deliver."

"How do you know that?"

"The whole thing would have been done by now."

"He's working on it with his father."

"Oh! And this charade is to get the man on board."

"At least there is something you don't know."

"At least I know that just as you're stuck on this illusory job, you're stuck on something else. For God's sake, you are carrying around a notebook in a child's handwriting. You must be stuck on something in your childhood … What is it?"

Elizabeth abruptly clammed up. She clutched her purse in the ready position to go home, stood up, realized the person to take her home wasn't there yet, and sat down. Both remained silent. Eventually most dancers needed a breather. The DJ's dance numbers could no longer get a crowd sashaying toward the dance floor, and the mainstay on the dance floor drifted off it because they were becoming an oddity. First Bode and Petite returned to the table, then Don.

"I have to go home," Elizabeth announced as soon as he sat down.

"Can't you wait till normal time?" asked Don as he dabbed his sweating face and neck with the lime handkerchief that matched his suit.

"Not tonight."

# CHAPTER 6

The dense pall of pollution that usually distorted the skies of that megacity during the day had a similar effect at night. From dusk to dawn, smog left its own cloud fully formed beneath celestial lights. Night after night, the smog cloud made the skies look like a region of thick smoke and made liars of meteorologists. When they reported of a crescent moon, no one without a telescope saw anything; when they swore of a full moon and the stars shining brightest, a deep gloom hung over the streets. Tonight, moonless and starless, a mountain of the deepest gloom sat all the way from the skies down to the ground.

Don's Mercedes S550 had left behind the well-lit A Avenue with its cacophonies of residential power generators and screeched onto an unlit street. He had been driving too fast, a little furiously, until he got to the twilight between the end of the lit street and the precipice of darkness on the other street when he slammed his brakes. Thus did the smell of burning rubber accompany the car as its tires dragged nosily on the road. Thereafter Don had to drive reasonably, for a stretch of compound walls higher than one floor on both sides of the narrow street and the blackened night created the illusion of driving in a tunnel. So he sat huffy in the car and filled it with hard silence.

Elizabeth's pulse inched up. She'd become worried that as soon as they reached the freeway she would get a grilling as a defendant in the case involving that other man.

They couldn't get to the freeway. Traffic had built up from the police checkpoint ahead to keep motorists at a standstill. Apparently, a lone ranger of a car-owner had refused to pay the bribe expected of him to pass police inspection of his car documents, and this had snowballed into a standoff. Drivers let their car engines idle and left their headlights on, signaling a momentary delay. Don, about ten cars to the checkpoint, had barely stopped before launching a tirade at the man: "Yes, he has to be different. Why not be like everybody else? Why not just give the police something for the weekend. No, he has to hold up everybody because he just doesn't want to get along. To just get with the program! People like that complicate other people's lives too. They must know that!"

Elizabeth got the distinct impression that Don's broadside was really an underhanded attack on her—a verbal subterfuge aimed at her. For inviting Gideon to the club, she had apparently bucked the program and so complicated Don's life. Yet she kept quiet. But she spoke up when he pressed onto his horns and other drivers joined him in filling the air with a racket of honking horns. "Stop!" she shouted to be heard.

Eventually he stopped. When the noise died down, he turned to her. "Why did you invite him?" he asked without preamble.

"I explained that when I told you about the invitation," she said, intentionally avoiding what he really wanted to know. He'd already heard about the man's sudden appearance, his attempt to get her to visit him and her deflection of it, and other factors of the invitation; now he wanted to know her real motive for the invitation, her motive deep down, only he had asked his question obliquely. And she had responded only to the surface aspect of his question because she needed time to find a way to proceed delicately. *I have to be sensitive to his feelings, but at the same time be clear I want nothing more serious than the relationship we have.*

He redirected her. "Do you like him?"

"You shouldn't be asking that."

"Why not? You can't even tell a friend if you like someone?"

"Okay," she said with equanimity. "He is likable, very likable. But he is too much for me."

"Likable, very likable?" he asked with suspicion.

"Truly unique. He just found me with so little information. He is very honest and straightforward. He simply took the keys of the flat and that was it—no games, no 'Come see me so you won't have to worry about the flat.'"

Don countered, "He can't make any trouble for that. At worst, I will pay the—"

"No, no, no—that's not what I mean," Elizabeth said quickly. "He just didn't try to exploit the situation. He could have tried. Everyone here tries to exploit every situation."

That stopped him for the moment. When his thoughts formed and he inched toward her to speak, he couldn't because all at once the honking racket had started again, this time without his lead or participation. He waited until the last sound to speak.

"So, do you like him?" he asked again with the stern air of a prosecutor determined to get an accused to confront the sole abiding question.

Elizabeth frowned. "Don," she said in a gruff voice, "I don't ask you such questions even though you run around with all these girls."

Don lost his patience too. "You could at least have taken him somewhere else," he snapped.

"So your special girlfriend won't suspect I have a boyfriend?" she asked rhetorically.

"What special girlfriend?" he asked with an incredulous air.

"The one always sitting near the staircase."

His tone became restrained. "Let's look at the big picture. Let's wait for Madam Agnes to finish working on my dad." He didn't add something Elizabeth would learn later, which was that part of his big picture had become to "pretend he could sustain a relationship with the one responsible girl in his life" (Madam Agnes's words) and, in so doing, regain a modicum of respect from a father exasperated with his son's frivolous friendships and frivolousness in general. "If you still want a job, I will still support you."

"Of course, I still want a job," she said.

"When I first promised to help—remember—I didn't ask you for anything."

"I respected you for that."

"So, just because of your small part in that girl's drama, you act like I killed somebody."

"You didn't kill anybody. You just disappointed me."

"You disappointed me, too. I mean, who does your boyfriend think he is?"

"He is not my boyfriend—he could have become a friend!"

"I don't see the difference."

"Stop being a hypocrite," she said firmly.

"Tell him, I buy drinks for top professors!"

"You were already acting strange before that."

"I expected somebody different."

"Why would you expect somebody different?"

"I expected somebody different, okay?" He shouted before he continued in a lower angry voice. "You just don't understand anything. Of course, he is very educated. He has to be likable, very likable. Yes, he is king of the world. He is the only angel in the sinful city of CDKuru."

"He is!"

"How is it that because I used you for a small thing, I have become a devil?" He wanted no answer now and waited for none as his anger and voice rose. "Devils don't drive around town—they enjoy themselves!"

#

The crude, searing heat of fury can easily short-circuit the brain. When fury surges wildly without pause, it shuts down the mind and inflames people into a crazed fit to do things they wouldn't ordinarily do—to, in a manner of speaking, unwittingly burn down their own homes.

Should Don later in life be introspective enough about his behavior when stalled with Elizabeth near the police checkpoint on that inauspicious Friday night, he would see his action there as dare-devilishly stupid. No—he did not ram his car through the police barricade to make himself and Elizabeth the target of a hail of police bullets. He had made a quick U-turn and driven recklessly fast as if he must return her to the club before something in her imploded his world.

Don's temper had worked against him again. The first time, his fury had made his tongue spew out that vow of never helping her again with employment. Had he restrained himself then and uttered just Madam Agnes's brief, Elizabeth would not have wandered away from his office to the vacant Proceedings flat for the chance encounter that led Gideon to the club tonight. This time, had he driven her home—even accusing her much of the way of forsaking good taste and good manners by inviting the other man—he would have at least kept Elizabeth and Gideon as apart as they were when she hurried off the club. And since those two had yet to establish a relationship, each could have been nonchalant about the other and stayed on his or her side of the divide—much to Don's benefit. Instead, out of anger, he united Elizabeth and Gideon; instead, Don dumped her on the lap of his perceived rival.

Hence, less than thirty minutes after the rash U-turn, Gideon had Elizabeth in his Honda Civic Sedan cruising toward the main street. He hadn't spoken since she asked at the club if he could take her home; he didn't even speak to her then—he merely got up, thrust his hand into his pocket to get out his keys, said a general "Good night" to those at the table, and led her to his car. She hadn't said anything else either. Their quiet company had been an easy one so far. She turned toward him and studied him for some time. When she got no reaction from him, she said, "Thank you."

"You are welcome."

"I owe you."

"Nothing owed. 'Thank you' is enough; the rest we chuck to humanity."

"If only everyone had your motto," she said with sudden vehemence. Her frustration was with the ways of CDKuru and with Don, who initially didn't want anything from her but had learned that nothing here came free. Charity was damned! For him to help arrange a job for her, at least she had to help him push off a bothersome lover. "Sometimes, I feel like a prey."

"Concrete jungle," he declared. "The decent are an endangered species."

"Yes," she concurred.

Their car reached A Avenue, turned left onto the street, and picked up speed. Traffic was light and visibility clear from the bright lights still supplied by the army of generators at the back or at the side of each house on that avenue.

With her frustration hacked from her chest and flung at the ubiquitous predators of CDKuru, she enjoyed the easy silence in the car until a thought lazed into her mind and lazed out. *The small lies we tell just to move life along.* The thought had come to her because of Don's lie to his friends after he and she returned to his table, sulking like two rain-drenched vultures, and faced curious stares. He could have ignored them—after all, the friends should have surmised that the two had quarreled about you-know-who. He didn't. He could have confirmed their conclusion—that would have been imprudent. Instead, he had said, "Too much traffic on the road." Elizabeth, glad then to see Gideon still sitting there, knew that he knew that the two hadn't returned to the club because of too much traffic—he knew full well that a lie had escaped Don's lips. She almost laughed. *Our friend here will not get with that type of program. He must have deducted points from Don's personality rating for that small lie.*

Gideon and Elizabeth had come near the confluence of A Avenue and the two streets leading to the freeway through different routes. She said, "Please, take T Street."

He answered, "Too many potholes there."

"There's a checkpoint on O Road," she said.

"No problem," he declared and stayed on the inside lane. He swung the car around the half-circle of the minor roundabout and continued straight onto O Road. Nothing else was said, but their silence remained agreeable. Not even the memory of her last drive on that street—the memory of her surly companion in that ride, the tense air in that car, and her taut nerves then—could bother her now. The memory had lost its fresh and poignant sentiments and felt abstract like a well-wrought picture evoking no emotions.

The checkpoint came into view. A large wick lamp atop a barrel in the center of the road highlighted crossbars stopping traffic and revealed the histrionic policeman on their side of the road. He was in a rifle shooting position, with the rifle aimed at their car. Nobody could mistake his message: speed off through the aperture after the barricade, and I'll hasten your exit to wherever dead people end up! Gideon had already started to ease to a stop. The car stopped and idled, its inside light on to facilitate the ineffectual nightly police hunt for armed robbers, for their weapons, and for their loot. Another police officer, gun slung over the shoulder, strolled over to the car.

Elizabeth, who usually shut her eyes in refusal to watch Don wangle his way through the checkpoint, found her eyes open and observing Gideon's interaction with the policeman, though her stomach had knotted in anxiety. Usually Don stopped at the barricade, said "Corporal [or whatever the rank of the sentry], hope you're having a good weekend," and held out the magic wad. As soon as the wad of money changed hands, the crossbar lifted. Thus, Don habitually passed checkpoints in just seconds.

The first time she saw him bribing cops, something inexplicable at the time happened to her. Out of nowhere, rage had streaked through her in the front seat of his car. Blazing heat

70

consumed her from head to toe. Her body quaked and her words came out in a shout when she tried to say, "Stop it! Stop giving them bribes!" Her outrage could not have been about this particular incident alone, for her shout had scathed as if born of a million grave injustices. She had startled herself. She had startled Don. She had startled the cop who left the money alone and said, "Please just go." Thereafter Don and Elizabeth unwittingly worked out a compromise: She would look away; he would do his business wordlessly. Only the "Thank you, sir" or any of the cop's obsequious farewells told her what had transpired.

Gideon retrieved his car documents from the glove compartment and tried to hand them to the cop. But the cop, a corporal, had sized up the car and its occupants (nothing in a 2012 Honda Civic and in two ordinarily dressed young adults screamed wealth and privilege) and decided he had an advantage. He was in no hurry now: He left his hands idle at the sides, left Gideon holding the documents aloft, and eyeballed the inside of the car and its occupants with all the indolence in the world. Finally his hand dragged up to receive the documents. A squat man with big head, wild eyes and scars-strewn face, he shone his torchlight on the first page, glanced at it, and dismissed it with loud derision. "My friend, photocopy is easy to forge," he shouted to soften Gideon up for a bribe. Then the cop barked, "I want the original!"

Gideon zinged back, "You don't expect anyone to carry around original documents in this place?"

He'd just stated the obvious. Only a stranger in the city or a fool would have a vehicle's original particulars anywhere within reach on a drive in that city rife with carjacking. Should he or she lose the originals and the car to armed robbers in one fell swoop, people who were usually sympathetic to robbery victims would mock the victim's stupidity endlessly. Yes, you could register every stolen car with papers in nearby states without any trouble at all. Yes, even if the carjackers were stupid or brazen enough to cruise around the neighborhood of the robbery in the stolen car—original license plate and color unchanged—and had the worst luck to be caught, they could engage their victim in a bribing contest for who gets to keep the car. That the extraordinary scope of police corruption (never mind their incompetence) matched that of the judiciary had forced car owners into locking their vehicles' original papers in the most secure vaults available at home. Gideon asked for the officer in charge.

"Just give me the original," the man said.

"Where is the officer in charge?" Gideon said again.

"Look at this man," complained the policeman. "Are you new here? You know what to do."

"Which is?"

"You are enjoying your weekend; we should enjoy our own too. Find us some small change and you can go."

"I really need to talk to your officer."

That got the corporal ranting and accusing Gideon of being a troublemaker. "You know what you are?" he asked at one point but continued without waiting for an answer. "You must know because you act like you know too much. Mr. I-Know-Too-Much! People like you get killed in this place. Do you hear me?"

"Okay," said Gideon nonchalantly.

"They get killed," the man bellowed to remind the unimpressed target of his tirade that this was talk of death and he should be afraid, should be shivering for being close to heaven's or hell's door.

"Just where is your officer?"

The corporal shouted toward Elizabeth: "Tell your husband to behave or I will go crazy!"

"You want him to give you money; he doesn't want to--"

"I don't think you heard me, Miss."

Gideon interjected quietly, "No need for all this. Get into the car—"

"No need for all that. We can do business out here."

"Get in so we can go settle this at your station."

The corporal said, "Who told you I want to go to the station? ... Miss, if you are my daughter, I won't allow you to marry him. He is a troublemaker. People like him don't do well here. Look at his car ... His mates are drinking Benz ... Mr. I-Know-Too-Much, get your cheap car away from here before I go crazy."

As Gideon drove away, Elizabeth felt an immense relief. "Thank you, thank you," she said to him.

"For what?"

"For calling his bluff."

"I won't take the easy way out and go along with something pernicious," he said. She felt a mild sense of unease and blocked out what he'd just said. She felt better. "It's happened before."

"Really?" she said. "This is my first."

"It was the same nonsense. The one I took to the superintendent in charge of the station got berated and couldn't return to the checkpoint that night. That meant he lost his cut of that night's bribes."

"Ha!" she said and echoed Shakespeare. "The unkindest cut of all."

Both of them burst into laughter.

# CHAPTER 7

Gideon drove fast through the fog of night and the occasional light toward I Road, the major freeway. They passed the sprawling Sheraton Hotel with its lights flooding out to the road and got within a mile of the freeway. Here, each of the hundred or so points of light from bush lamps revealed a delicacy stand on ground level on both sides of the road. Chicken, peanut-flavored kebabs, fried snails, black-eyed pea fritters, meat pies, and venison beckoned from glass containers or the meats sizzled atop small grills. Soda and water sellers carried their wares on the head or arms trotting back and forth to hustle out the last penny from customers in cars before closing shop that day.

"Do you want some snacks?" he asked.

"No, thanks," she said.

She'd been stealing glances him since the corporal's hasty retreat from a ride to the station, stared at Gideon when they drove through darkness but averted her eyes when they came under floodlights. She'd believed that her continual staring at him was just an idle venture in the car, that since he had not said much she couldn't chatter on or simply keep staring out of the window. Nevertheless, by the time she gave up on her coy attention to him after assuming that he must have become aware of it, a mystical force had possessed her. Fabulous perceptions had become possible. Suddenly Gideon's stature had grown exponentially before her very eyes. One second he had human stature; the next he had demigod stature. He was now the most important man—no, the most important person—in the whole wide world. You'd think he had just discovered the vaccine for cancer.

How utterly different her response to him was! She'd never found herself staring like that at Don or even thinking of him in that way. Elizabeth didn't know why then—she knew little then of these types of things. She would know more, later, on hearing Big Mama's treatise on the absence of love: "No guru has to tell you anything because nothing really happens to you. It's skin-deep and out there. He can't awaken the unique spirit buried deep, deep in your soul. Nothing profound will pass between you two. You may learn to be with him. With time and patience, you may even become happy with him if he is a decent man. That will be it—happy but never blissful." In a way, Big Mama wanted Elizabeth to think of the wrong man as a dead battery in a car. Turn the car key on and nothing ignites. No sparks fly. Of course, you can always jumpstart the car.

Elizabeth, sitting right there in the car, could not have articulated her feelings for Don in terms of "skin-deep and out there" and nothing really happening to her, though she felt as much. As for Gideon, she had not fully felt the "bliss" yet, even though in her instinctive comparison of the two men at this time, Gideon would still get infinite points for touching her heart, while Don got zero or something close. A mathematician, intoxicated or not, would have judged the contest a technical knockout, with Don having lost the match too hopelessly for a rematch. However, the logic of math doesn't always square with human motives.

The Honda entered the expressway. A dual carriageway of five lanes each way, I Road was an easy thoroughfare to enter. Its two outside lanes were more or less service lanes with sturdy median at strategic locations to curtail traffic on the outside lanes and make merging onto the freeway from side streets manageable. The car zipped onto the road, south toward the city center, with such burst that the usually inert air of CDKuru rushed into the cabin. She gasped, and he immediately closed the windows with the automatic switch.

Then it happened. She wasn't even looking at him when a sublimely comforting tonic filled her up and cocooned her in bliss. She became as relaxed as could be, as secure as could be, and enraptured by a unique sensation that filled up her world. Tender, tender, tender she felt, losing herself completely in the experience, seeing him without looking as everything else faded completely from her mind in that ecstatic eclipse that had blanked out anything that had to do with the past or the future—anything that had nothing to do with the duo at this exact moment.

#

At home she was awake and spellbound on the bed. The novel sensations she had felt in the car from I Road all the way to the front gate of Irnopi would not fade in the room. The magic and the bliss remained in the air. He remained the sole presence in her head—not his looks, his attitudes or any such definable attribute, but his spirit. And what a magnificent spirit it was! Her heart strummed the rapturous music of love. Love? She didn't recognize the spell on her as love—she didn't try to place it. She knew she felt great. Great! That was it. End of story. But that was not the end of the story for her subconscious. It noted the affinity between him and her and started reacting.

Consequently, that old surreal feeling came over her again. The image of gushing blood entered her mind and a cry looped with a scream echoed in her head. Panic—currents of it—shot through her. Her body began to boil from high-grade fever. Her lungs and chest constricted as if she'd inhaled fumes. She had to gasp for breath. The scream faded off, leaving the cry to pierce the night. She half-thought that the cry was inside her as well as outside her. Her palms clamped over her ears to silence the auditory disturbance, pushing harder and harder into the ears without achieving her goal. Finally she cried out to release her torment to the room.

"Elizabeth!" Big Mama called from the other room. Elizabeth didn't respond. She hadn't fully recovered herself yet. Besides, she sensed that the call was meant to wake her up from a nightmare. The old woman didn't know that Elizabeth wasn't having the usual type of nightmare. The night became quiet again.

Suddenly she started remembering that day in first grade when she felt the wicked lash of a child's tongue. "You don't have a mother because you are evil," the classmate had told Elizabeth more than a decade and a half ago. Both of them had been on recess, idling on a sandy ridge near the soccer field. How both of them ended up at that spot remained a mystery to Elizabeth since something in each of the girls always pointed them in opposite directions—if the girl went left, Elizabeth went right; if the girl went south, Elizabeth went north. The geometry from the girls' intuition ensured they never met at a point, except in the classroom, where the teacher, Mrs. Udu, kept all students quiet as a mouse and kept the inexplicable rivalry between the two girls an unspoken one.

That day, the students had taken another test to determine each student's rank in the class. Mrs. Udu had, as she said, corrected the papers, tallied the points, and compiled the list. "I will post the list during recess," she had said. "For now, here is your last test." But students, anxious to know their rankings, had congregated in her front door after the bell for recess. She ordered them off that area, and they all left.

On the sandy ridge, a group of girls milling around with Elizabeth told her they thought she was going to remain the best in the class. She hesitated out of modesty, and a sharp voice cut through her hesitation. "No, I am going to be first," the girl said.

"No, I am going to be first," Elizabeth rejoined.

"I have ninety-five percent," the girl gloated.

"I have hundred percent," Elizabeth said emphatically.

The group began laughing at the girl; she glared at Elizabeth and yelled at her those horrendous words—the worst cutting words that anyone could utter to a motherless child.

The world of those little girls had stood still in shocked silence. Then the commotion started. Elizabeth lost complete control of herself, tore into the girl with such demonic fury it took two male teachers to pull her away from the prostrated girl weeping on the sand pile. The adults, too, on hearing the details of the incident were shocked by what the girl had said of Elizabeth, and even Mrs. Udu, who was usually firm but reserved, had lost her composure for a moment and tried to pinch the loud mouth permanently shut.

But the genie had escaped, and the whole incident crystallized Elizabeth's primal fears of being a demon child. First, an invisible monster had possessed her, boiled her blood high enough to keep her frenzied, and infused her legs and hands with enough violent energy to almost kill that girl. Second, Elizabeth saw her situation of being the only child without a mother in the town and in her school as proof of something vile in her, especially given the nature of her mother's death. Yet, right after the incident, Elizabeth couldn't think of it or bring it up with her father or caregiver—she tried to forget the incident, to bury it. This was when she began to delude herself with the idea that in fact she had a living mother and that her caregiver fit that bill. Even after the woman left to get married, Elizabeth still couldn't revisit that incident.

Tonight, however, the incident had, for the first time since its occurrence in her childhood, burst into the open.

Time was around twelve, and in Irnopi, this was really the dead of night since darkness came around six and—without electricity to prolong the day—ushered people almost immediately to bed. At this time, the ebony night had cast the spell of sleep on the children on their mats on the floor and on the occupants of the other room. Elizabeth tried to sleep too. Instead, she found herself thrashing around the bed, for every way and everywhere she tried to rest her body on the bed felt awkward, and she continued to seek the elusive combination of a comfortable sleeping posture and the right spot on the bed to help her sleep. Yes, the heat induced her sweat to flow freely, and female mosquitoes, out for blood, circled endlessly for the opportune time to stick their needles into her body, but she couldn't have slept anyway had that room been bereft of those two problems. That belligerent childhood memory had stimulated her nerves—stimulated nerves heralded insomnia.

With her eyes wide open in the pitch-black midnight hour of Irnopi, Elizabeth felt rattled again. She shivered now because the memory she'd escaped for more than fifteen years came back tonight to haunt her. She shivered now because of the way the image of gushing blood got to her tonight. No, she hadn't breached any of her don'ts on the survival guide she'd developed over the years. Her mind didn't wander toward the dreadful topic. She didn't listen to the combination of words that usually ignited to trigger her memories. No. Nothing. Yet she got the image suddenly in her mind. And as suddenly she'd found herself remembering the dreadful incident. *Something new triggered these. What is it?*

Whatever the cause, it had left Elizabeth guileless and therefore naked to the cold fact that she'd been running away from all her life. Her temperature dropped precipitously. Her sweat and bed felt arctic cold—cold as if the bed with her in it had switched location from that hot room in the slum to a mortuary. She immediately curled up like a fetus in the womb, pulling the bed sheet over her body for warmth.

#

The next day, in an interlude in CDKuru's blackout, the single clear bulb washed the room with light as the ceiling fan creaked on to maintain a breeze.

Elizabeth had prepared for a session of work on her hair. She had lifted the center table onto the bed to create space for a small wooden stool and for her to stretch out her legs. Now she sat hunched on the stool, her legs crossed toward the door. The braids at the back of her head came undone, one at a time in the hands of Big Mama, who sat hunched on the settee as she pried loose with a comb the braid in her hand. "Thank you," Elizabeth said.

"Must you thank me for everything?" Big Mama joked. "Send the thanks to the person who gave us electricity just now."

Usually, a joke or quip spurred small talk between the

women. Today it didn't: Elizabeth, with lips pressed together, uttered no repartee. Her mood was somber, had been for a while—except when she, along with others in the neighborhood, raised a cheer to the restored electricity. As such, as she sat on the stool, her face wore a somber look, and her entire demeanor was of withdrawal into troubled silence.

Though both women shared no genes, they felt the kinship of an older, wiser sister to a much younger one who needed guidance. They shared confidences, trust, and much else. Now, with Big Mama seeing herself in the role of protector, she hated it when Elizabeth started shutting down on her and so had to maneuver to open up her charge's locked lips.

First, Big Mama tried the obvious. In a comforting tone, she addressed Elizabeth for a while about keeping her joblessness in perspective. "Yes," Big Mama eventually concluded, "someone without hope can sometimes feel like the end of the world has come. You should not. You have survived so far; you will continue to survive until your luck gets you a job. Stop punishing yourself over something you can't control."

When the speech failed to get a word out of the charge— failed to get anything but somber silence—Big Mama tried to provoke a reaction, any kind of reaction. She mused that just when she was starting to worry that Elizabeth was waiting too long to be seduced, the girl tied herself up with two men. Laughing, Big Mama continued, "I have heard of being lucky in love, but I did not know that it meant two lovers at one time."

Still Elizabeth kept her mouth shut. Though she was tempted to respond, with a response already formed in her mind because the old woman had uncannily cut close to the crux of the matter, Elizabeth resisted—the matter was too grave for that seriocomic tone, so she maintained her troubled silence. Big Mama gave up being circumspect, left the braids alone for a moment, and asked directly, "What is troubling you?"

Like a discharging cannon, Elizabeth fired off her concern in the form of a question. "How do you know the wrong man?" she asked. The wrong man here meant someone for just a casual affair—someone to date for dating sake. Yet she actually wished to know about the opposite kind of man, the kind that engendered an enduring relationship. But when you are scared of something, you don't leap toward it. You dither and dither and circle around it—you can always hear bad news later?

Big Mama heaved a sigh and moped for some time. When she regained herself, she spoke carefully—her tone drawling with resignation. She spoke of the dull spirit he evoked in you … of the absolute necessity for something external—be it fame, good looks, wealth, prosperity—to camouflage at least for some time the failure of two souls to mate. "An unmistakable reluctance will overcome you," she pronounced and paused.

Suddenly addressing the opposite kind of man, Big Mama said, "No guru will tell you when you find the right man."

"Wait!" Elizabeth shouted. "Keep talking about the wrong man."

"Instead of the dull—"

"Wait! Wait!"

"You have to hear it now, Elizabeth … Instead of the dull and empty feeling you have for the wrong man, you will get a unique inspiration from the right man. You will feel contented in a quiet way. You will feel the world of peace inside. Your soul will settle like a wanderer who has finally found a real home."

Elizabeth's hope against hope started to fizzle. She said,

"The quote unquote right man for you is the wrong man for me."

"You can run and hide from the truth, but that doesn't change it ... Everybody needs the special connection that nourishes the soul. And if you are lucky enough to find that with a man and lose him, regret will be yours. Every now and then you will pine for that wonderful connection."

Elizabeth slumped. Her desperate hope for Gideon to qualify as a man destined for a casual affair with her had dashed to pieces. She had hoped to hear love defined and described in a way that did not sound like the emotion that had filled her up in the car with him. She had hoped to hear of love not as a serene experience, but as an exciting and excitable one with trumpets, bells, and whistles. She had hoped to hear of love the way Hollywood portrayed it. Instead, Big Mama had spoken about love's serene nature and had proceeded to let her tongue lecture about the occasional horror of lost love—about the horror of lost love! *I know very much about the horror of lost love. I have avoided love my entire life—avoided it like a plague—because I do not want to worry about losing that love. One bad news has followed another. I should not have asked that question.*

In frustration, Elizabeth lashed out by asking, "If what you just said is your last word on the matter, do you regret marrying your husband?" Immediately she wished she could retract the question, for it was loaded. It was asking Big Mama (in the context of their discussion) to choose between her beloved that she didn't marry and the husband she seemed to have grown fond of—her husband with whom she'd gone through life's trials and tribulations and had four children. But the question had already worked its way through the air to Big Mama's ears.

The old woman drew a sharp breath. Then she mulled the question quietly, shifted in her seat, took hold of a braid and said, "Bend a little more so I can see the root of the braid in my hand." After the neck bent a little, silence subsumed the two for some time. Eventually, Big Mama said, "I can't say 'yes,' and I can't say 'no.' Yes, I regret not marrying that other man. When I hear his name, I imagine what could have been, and I miss the special feeling I had in his company in those days. But to say 'yes' will mean to be without my children—you know, without my husband, these very children would not have been born. So I can't fantasize about any life for me without my children and their father."

In effect, maternal love reigned supreme despite all she'd said about the other kind of love. It kept her from playing this game of being in her twenties again and having to rechoose her spouse, of having to choose between her childhood sweetheart and the man she married. Her occasional fantasy for her first love didn't really alter much. She could not unequivocally choose him over her husband because that would entail her having to wipe out, at least in her thoughts, the existence of these children. Big Mama was unwilling to do so even for the sake of an argument.

Elizabeth's petulant attempt to make Big Mama see that her own life contradicted her expressed views on love had bogged down in the swamp of an old mother's emotional response. So Elizabeth's main problem remained and she could no longer avoid it. She could no longer turn deaf to all the molecules in her body whispering she'd fallen in love. Now that Big Mama had forcefully confirmed it in her own way, forces seen or unseen emblazoned "You are in love" in Elizabeth's mind. She started thinking. *I was right about love. I was fine when I stayed away from it. The moment I swooned for him, I saw that vision of blood again and remembered the horrible incident I had not remembered in all these years ...*

Soft hands and comb had gone back to teasing her braids loose. The hushed aftermath of the women's sobering heart-to-heart remained in the air, and the fan continued to squeak and shatter the silence in the room. A short while later, the sound ceased, the electric bulb's wire filament no longer glowed, and the room became dingy. Electricity had come and gone. Now Big Mama had to continue her task with her fingers feeling their ways into the matted hairs to untangle them.

She did so quietly, steering the head to suit her purpose. This suited Elizabeth's mood—this lack of oral directions. She needed silence and solitude to mull over her new situation, especially at this opportune time that the bar in the opposite house hadn't started blaring loud music and the usual community noise of too many active people in that overcrowded compound and slum hadn't started. She needed her mind to concentrate on what to do now about her situation with Gideon. She had promised to visit him on Tuesday. At the time of the promise, she believed in a simple world—a world of one dimension, a world in which her heart hadn't conjoined a man's heart and started compounding issues for her. *No! Nothing is simple. One thing here complicates another thing over there. One serene experience in a car with a man—just one—and I learn that I am in love. One short ride and I see that vision—one short ride and off I go on a dangerous memory lane ... The casual affair with Don is far better than this serious intrusion into my psyche ... Now, what am I to do to end it?*

86

She pondered the question. Finally she posed a question to herself. *Why not abandon Tuesday's promised visit and hope he takes the hint to leave me alone?*

## CHAPTER 8

By Tuesday, however, Elizabeth knew she would visit him even if her doubts turned into human form, grew the muscles of giants, and pulled her back every step of the way. At first, she told herself she had to be there at the least; after all, she had promised. But as the hours counted down to leaving her house, she had an embarrassed laugh at her own expense because she'd started to feel quite enthralled by the visit and to wish that time passed quicker so she could see him soonest.

That mid-morning, Elizabeth abandoned her usual bland look for casual elegance. A touch of lipstick and clothes her size did the magic. The clothes—a beige short-sleeve blouse and a knee-length batik skirt with patterns of clustered burgundy hearts embedded on black lattice—fitted well that eyes could make out her shapely figure. She'd parted her hair in two, brushed it to her shoulder, and matted each side to the tip. This elegance would expose her to amorous eyes on the streets, she knew. *Those useless men will bother me today. But I don't care.*

She didn't care when —within shouting distance of her compound—a completely bald old man with a jutting rubbery face stopped maneuvering his garish white Mercedes Benz 190E back and forth between the two side gutters to try to decoy Elizabeth to a bedroom with the usual "Miss, where are you going?" In the past, such crude efforts and the street audience had always embarrassed her. Today she had a new lover's enchanted aura. She felt removed from all of that and retained as much of a relaxed gait as chipped heels would allow. She even felt light-hearted about the man and his kind as she floated away

toward W Avenue. *Why won't they go after girls who like them?*
*Why me? I don't want potbellied men. I don't want bald old men*
*with stained teeth. Yes, I'm too respectful to say that to them, but*
*I've heard some angry girls tell such men at one time or the*
*other that they are just too old or too ugly to be romantic figures.*

At Akala Bus Stop, the conductor of a revving Kombi
chanted "Oro Idi! Oro Idi!" He was actually going to Nihsum,
but was exploiting the scheme of terminating his journey at the
midway point of Oro Idi to wheedle more money out of hapless
passengers. "Nosnawal! Nosnawal!" chanted another conductor.
She could hop into either bus for the first leg of her journey. But
this choice was not between two good routes or even between a
good one and a bad one—it was a choice between Scylla and
Charybdis. The Nosnawal route was longer, byzantine, and
fraught with unreliable bus connections between stops. The
Nihsum route was shorter, straightforward and inviting with
frequent bus connections between stops—however, Elizabeth
had stepped foot at Nihsum once and vowed, "Never again."

She hopped into the Oro Idi bus without thinking.

#

Anyone who wants to see magic in action should watch
a person newly in love. In Elizabeth's case, she heard melodies
that no one else in the bus heard. Her spirits soared, and she felt
alive, joyful, free and in the moment. She had forgotten her vow
of never passing through Nihsum again—all she had in mind was
Gideon, Gideon, Gideon. His spirit had so preoccupied her that
she turned her gaze inward and saw everyone and everything on
the streets through eyes filmed over with distraction.

She hardly noticed as her bus navigated through the
rowdy scenes that constricted A Rotom Road at Oro Idi and

reached the area of the road where contractors who skimped on adequate tar and soil to pay bribes had done their shoddiest work. She hardly noticed the slow and unsteady drive through this area where cleaved earth effectively closed part of the road and left the remaining part with arbitrarily strewn jagged potholes, sinkholes and trenches. Even a sanguine person would have muttered a prayer when the bus tilted up and down and jerked through a ditch in that zone. She was in her own world the entire time.

At Nihsum, however, the tenor of life jarred her awake. Bedlam and riotous sensations threatened to swallow their bus. An open market that sprawled on both sides of A Rotom Road, six bus stops in proximity, and a million souls at cross-purposes jammed the entire space. Roaring and howling noises pounded the eardrums when she, along with other passengers, disembarked before the bus stop. A short walk later, she faced the bedlam and babel of throaty ware hawkers and hagglers, of noisy horns from a million automobiles and of blaring sound systems. There, the wild noise reached its crescendo.

Tarrying on the roadside to work up her courage to brave through the core of this area, Elizabeth realized she was losing herself. She had practically sleepwalked to a place where she'd suffered one of the most disorienting experiences of her life and had shunned, logging extra miles on routes that steered her clear of this hades. But today, with all that hosannas in the air because of her date with Gideon, she had lost track of her fear of the place. Suddenly she remembered why she had fled Nihsum.

It was her first time there, and the place had been maddeningly surreal. An airtight density of people for blocks on end had opened up before her eyes, life whirled everywhere as madding crowds jostled onto the roads and off in alarm because motor vehicles tried to muscle through and packs of commuters tore through other crowds to hop onto smoke-belching buses that slowed but kept moving. The ceaseless trooping of all humanity back and forth on the roads commingled with other forms of chaos—all of these fired with maniac energy.

The commotion had assaulted her senses to a ten on a scale of ten. Her prior experiences with overcrowding in concerts, in stadium, and in student demonstrations against one thing or the other hadn't prepared her for the riotous noises exploding continuously in her ears or for the ceaselessly frenetic motion of the sea of people in all directions threatening to close in on her any minute. Her senses had been overloaded as if her head had opened up and every chaotic sensation poured in. She couldn't distinguish where her thoughts and actions stopped from where those of others began. She thought she was going mad or getting crushed alive. Her instinct was to run away; she couldn't in that place. She'd stopped moving. A mistake! An onrushing crowd of more than a hundred closed in on her from all sides, herding her along into a bus that had slowed in front of her. A wrong bus for her, she didn't fight the seismic momentum. Survival instincts had kicked in and she had chosen riding a wrong bus a short distance over trying to push through a frenzied crowd that would leave her eviscerated and disheveled.

Elizabeth's remembrance of the dreadful experience there last time—her mind's replay of the key features of that experience—made her able to imagine Nihsum's fantastic scope of things without fearing that she might be hallucinating. Now she could—and did—immerse her mind in the sights and sounds of the place. Something became apparent to her: the place had no full-blown riot on its hands—the crowds had the uncanny sense to remain perpetually on the verge of stampede. Elizabeth lost her dread of the place and became calm and collected in the middle of that maelstrom. So, without a thought about where she was, she moved toward the infinite horde of people in her way. She found gaps in their midst, sidled through some, sidestepped or paused when they closed rapidly, and maneuvered every limb in her body, like a contortionist, to pick her way through one throng after another for half a mile to the Proceedings Road Bus Stop. Not once did she flinch as she pushed through a place she'd pegged as too disorienting to enter.

#

After she arrived at Gideon's apartment, settled down in the living room and made small talk for a while, he said, "That notebook."

"Yes?"

"Were you practicing your handwriting and just copying words?"

"No," she said and stopped. He waited for an explanation. She burst into laughter. "Who's asking leading questions now?"

He laughed too. "You've got me."

"No, I've got you back."

"Right again."

Then she said, "My father was talking; I was taking dictation."

"How old were you then?"

"I'm not sure. But I remember I was in early elementary grade—maybe second or third grade. We had read and reread all the books we had. We couldn't get any new books, so he started to improvise and that was it."

"I keep remembering the page on valleys and oceans."

"Why that page?"

"The book just opened to … What's wrong with that page?"

"It's about love."

"Love?"

"How deep it is and how one can't fully convey it."

"He must have been quite a lover."

"A tragic lover." Then she changed the subject. "He loved the classics."

"Did you follow his footsteps?"

"He wanted me to have 'functional degrees, marketable degrees'—accountancy, accountancy, accountancy. But here I am without a job." She kept her thoughts from going farther into the cruel irony and studied the room.

It was furnished with simple chic. A living room set of velvet green chaise longue for one, a love seat, and a settee flanked a burgundy carpet and faced the entertainment center—a gleaming dark wood unit with space for a 55-inch flat screen television and several shelves for the components of the audio stereo set. Two side tables and a coffee table—all ovals from the wood of the entertainment center—complemented the seats. The same wood and shape carried over to the dining area. There, the elliptical dark dining table and its four chairs stood on another burgundy carpet, with matching China cabinet at the corner as backdrop.

Both of them hushed for a minute. He watched her. She sipped his brew of Fanta and Coke. Between sips of the tasty drink, she scanned the place repeatedly. Despite power outage, she felt cool and saw everything there. She gave the casual, swanky, airy feel of the furnished apartment a silent applause. *Yes. That's it. Yes!* Elizabeth could not have picked these particular pieces of furniture, but since the first day she stepped into the flat, she had envisioned for it a stylishly casual, comfortable and fluid decor—the very effect Gideon had achieved there. "Nice," she said. "Nice."

"Thanks," he replied. He stood up from the love seat to move the coffee table an inch toward her, though to reach it wouldn't have been a stretch for Elizabeth. Apparently, the serious light-skinned man dressed in green polo shirt, khaki pants, and slippers wanted life much, much easier for the woman sitting on the settee in his living room. "If you can bear the noise, I will turn on the generator for you," he said.

"Oh no!" she said. "Everything is fine."

He remained standing a while longer, studying her with concern. Finally he asked her, "The job arrangement still stalled?"

"Yes."

"Push things. Go straight to the man in the shadow."

"Straight to his father?"

"Yes."

"What if that makes him just say 'no'?"

"Because you went directly to him?"

"People like him want things done through back channels. I just have to wait."

He paused to study her for a moment, before saying, "My main concern is your welfare. How do you feel?"

His words and especially his genuine concern triggered her emotions. Despair mingled with shame—the despair of tramping around for a non-existent job and the shame of being a failure and a parasite. Her heart grew heavy, and all she could do was to shrug her shoulders wordlessly in a gesture of defeat. As she did so, her face wore a dull shrunken look and her eyes filled up with the sorrow of a million injustices. He came over to the settee, sat next to her, and took her hand. Right away, she began to feel the soft and soothing power of his palms.

Gradually, time—as they say—stood still. Clocks must have stopped ticking. Earth must have stopped orbiting the sun. Only one ever-expanding moment of stillness prevailed. An utterly relaxed moment, it stretched on and on. How long of clock time did this last? Thirty minutes? One hour? Two? Neither of them could say even at the penalty of death. What should be noted, though, was that as the sun cast a longer shadow on the building, the soothing sensations from his hands to her hand flowed to other parts of her body, washed away the anguish in her heart and mind, and made her entirely calm. Elizabeth felt settled and safe—ensconced in a transcendent state, in a timeless world, in heaven. Her mind had become lucid enough and her heart magnanimous enough to find the world, including the harsh details of her present situation, in simple harmony.

But moments of pure harmony with one's world are rare. Many have lived and died without experiencing a single moment of that grace. Rarer still is a prolonged experience of such harmony. A mere mortal, Elizabeth's moment of grace eventually evaporated in that parlor. She returned to daily concerns, to the usual preoccupation with the ordinary aspects of life, to being curious about him.

This was when Gideon's past came into play. "You

know what they say of balanced equations," she said with an embarrassed laugh. "Each side has an equal number of atoms."

He laughed too as he said, "You mean I know more about you than you—"

"Yes," she said, before adding, "I can't hide much from you. I have to try harder."

"I'll tell you all you want to know about me. Just ask."

She faced an awkward moment and fumbled for a minute for a question. "Why are you on sabbatical?"

"I have a grant to explore things that make marriages an economic force."

"Of all things, why that?"

"Well, I grew up hearing stories of how my mother helped my father—I mean my stepfather. Before his marriage, he had a good income but he was a big spender. I heard a lot of talk about his lavish ways in his bachelor days and the fact that he had nothing to show for all the money he made. Once married, he built a few homes. He became a sensible investor."

"Was your thesis on that?"

"No, my thesis was about how modern cities at an embryonic stage—CDKuru today and Tammany NY in the 1920s—can develop suffocating corruption."

"That's more academic. Your study seems to have a functional purpose."

"It does."

"Why are they sponsoring a study of this place?"

"The sponsors are trying to address poverty in developing countries."

"Oh!"

Both fell silent. Then Elizabeth picked up the

conversation. "How far?"

"All I've done is what I did before stepping into this country."

"Nothing in months?"

"Nothing."

"Why not?"

A sudden solemn mood afflicted him.

# CHAPTER 9

Gideon's eyes stared off into space and he remained immobile and silent for some time. The atmosphere had become eerie. Then he began quietly the tale of his life after his mother's death.

The father had gone to pieces. He kept hearing his dead wife's voice calling him as if to tell him something and only after he'd answered the calls would he realize she was already dead. Gideon decided he had to move the man out of the house he'd shared with the wife and move him to where he'd get filial company. An empty house full of memories of the couple's life together would throw up ghosts for the surviving spouse, Gideon reasoned. So he sought a visa for the man. Part of the visa process involved a DNA test to prove they were father and son. Unfortunately, unholy of unholies, the result of the test upended the lives of the erstwhile biological father and son. Gideon, who could not awaken his mother to pry out of her the identity of his biological father, became ensnared in trying to sort himself out.

"Sorry," she said in a horrified tone. "Sorry."

He recovered a little to say, "You didn't know." His eyes hooded with sadness, and his hands, now lifeless on her hand, conveyed defeat. Eventually he said, "Her relatives won't help. They stall and stall, and so I know nothing much of what might have happened." His lips locked, and his gloom and silent torment seemed to deepen. She cupped her hands around his and comforted him while they sat struck silent.

The past had willed itself into the present. Horror from the past filled the thoughts of the young man and young woman with the lacerating pain of the pulled crust of a deep wound. The room felt haunted—it filled up with eerie silence. His temperature spiked—his body burning with the sickly searing heat of fever. Her body stuck to his—feeling his fever anywhere their bodies touched, especially on her palms and on her side. She knew that he needed her unspoken sympathy and that letting her body absorb the heat would provide succor to him. She found herself so caught up in that emotional moment she believed it was her fate to save him from his ghosts. After a while, his fever subsided. His hands and side again began to feel naturally warm to Elizabeth.

The faint echo of the honking of a car entered the room, as did the urgent chirping of birds. Near the gate, the compound guard's radio came on speaking an obscure foreign language. Gideon and Elizabeth knew power had returned. He got up, walked to the large sliding glass door, closed it without drawing the blind, and turned on the ceiling fan. Life had returned to its normal grind, and the handholding didn't continue when he returned to his seat. He sat there, one arm on the shoulder of the settee, the other hand in his pocket.

She clasped her hands on her lap. *I should not have started this discussion. All I had expected were the ordinary facts of life—I had no idea he had such a burden.* "Sorry," she said again.

"For what?"

"For starting this discussion."

"I would have told you one way or the other."

Relieved that she hadn't unwittingly caused him to access a no-go area of his memory, she realized now that clues about this horrible incident had been before her eyes from his first conversation with her to a recent one. The first time both spoke, he'd said, "my father, former father"; a few minutes before the bombshell, he had again mischaracterized his relationship with the man only to correct himself ("my father— my stepfather"). She wondered about the man and looked askew.

Gideon saw the look. "What's the question?" he asked. When she hesitated, he added, "I know you have a question. Just ask it."

"What about the man?"

"No, he hasn't died from shock. He has become lucid and moved to the village."

"Do you visit him often?"

"I saw him once—that was it."

"He is as much a victim—"

"I know, I know. But when I saw him, I pictured them together, a couple, and everything started tumbling in my mind."

"You have to learn to compartmentalize. Break things up. Stop making connections. That's dangerous."

"I can't. I see how the pieces are linked."

"I do too—just not when it is something horrible. You just have to build a firewall around each piece so that one can't link to another in your mind."

#

Don's driver had come twice for Elizabeth that Tuesday, and Don himself had come after work to impress on her, through Big Mama, that "there is great news."

One message from the driver would have been enough. Elizabeth would not allow a repeated mishap—she would not let another job slip through her fingers. She awoke early the next day to shower, put on a tie-dye maternity dress, and sit on the settee in the grayish Irnopi room until a proper time to visit an office. Hope inflated a small part of her heart. Big Mama tried to dampen expectations. She said, "Hope is good and bad. It allows us to carry on, but it also gets us disappointed. Somebody without hope does not get disappointed. Do all you can, but don't get your hopes high. If these people wanted to give you the job today, Donald would have been the first person to come here for you. A driver does not bear the glorious message."

Elizabeth's pocket of hope started a slow leak. By the time she sat down in Don's office, she was solemn.

If he noticed the look, he didn't bring it up. He himself lacked his characteristic cheer. Though he had smiled his welcome, the smile did emerge from a solemn face with pleading eyes. Dressed in elegant dark blue suit, white shirt, and burgundy tie with light blue and white stripes, Don was nervous.

"Donald, what's the great news?" she asked.

They were sitting in the business area—she on a guest seat, he on his chair. Carefully watching her, he stood up, came around the table to her side, and told her, "Let's sit over there." He led the way to the lounge area, where he waited for her to sit before sitting. Then he stood up and took the extraordinary step of locking the door before he took off his jacket and hung it on a nearby hanger.

Elizabeth knew now that the answer to her question wouldn't delight her. Otherwise, he would have blurted it out as soon as she'd stepped into his office. He had qualified good news for her: the "yes, but" kind of good news; something to the effect that his dad had set things up for her but … She sensed that an unpleasant request was sticking to Don's tongue. Already, her affair with him seemed more serious to the world than she would have liked. She had also played that huge role in his sly exit from his ex-queen. Now what?

She knew she ought to take a stand. She knew she ought to say "no more" and walk away, but her retrospective of her job odyssey made her feel like someone lost in a wilderness like the Sahara, like a blind waddling in sand dunes to nowhere. A thought crossed her mind. *At least I have gotten closer to a job with Don.* So she remained in her seat but couldn't prod him for an answer. She simply sulked, wishing he dithered on and on before speaking, for she suddenly lost the resolve to object to whatever was forthcoming as long as it had a glimmer of hope. Yet as she waited for him to find a way to spin the news positively, she had to numb and inoculate herself against the outcry from her soul to abandon the entire enterprise now.

"There is a way people get on here," he began, watching her and still pleading with his eyes. "Use what you have to get what you want. That's it. You are a friend, even more than a friend to me. You have to let me help you. We are lucky dad wants to help, but he wants you to join the family on Sunday. I know how you feel. Don't worry …"

The old man had thrown her a curved ball. She had expected that whenever he got back to her, he would ask or direct that she came escorted to his office. Instead, he wanted her in his home, on a Sunday no less. Anyone who knew the man knew he spent Mondays to Saturdays in diabolical circles with other dealmakers. He spent Sundays in church, where he couldn't help seeing other worshippers, and at home with the closest members of his already small clique. "It's only when dad has a very, very important deal that he allows someone else into the house on Sundays," Don had once told Elizabeth.

"Otherwise, he gave all his time to God and to his family."

She had no inkling of what moved the man to send the message, no inkling of why he wanted her in his home on a Sunday, still she felt entirely uneasy about the invitation. For one lucid moment, the voice of her conscience warned her. *You are at the point of no return. Say no!* An alternative scenario suggested itself. *Maybe I should go to his office, instead. Maybe I should ask if I could come to his office instead.* She swallowed hard, for her life's vast bleakness started to close in on her. Her thoughts forcefully reminded her of her jobless hard life: her freeloading in the slum dwelling, her constant horror of being penniless, the daily slights and humiliations she got from anyone who could slow down her suffering, her feeling of being a zombie and a sly beggar ... She succumbed fully to a bleak vision of her present and her future.

Her survival instinct kicked in. She began to parse the invitation for the glimmer of hope, for any kind of hope. Something flickered in her mind. *At least, the man wants to meet me.* That sounded to her like a giant step toward receiving the employment letter. Suddenly she lost her dubious feeling about the invitation. In fact, she felt better about it. The thought of asking to go to his office instead of his house vanished. Her sneaky suspicion that any version of a negative response from her could send her to the back of an ever-swelling pool of millions of job applicants evaporated. She had conned herself into suspecting no malign intent in the whole thing—so, she kept mum about the invitation.

Don paused in surprise. In the past, each time he'd implied a serious relationship between them, she'd gone an extra mile to correct the impression—yet today's invitation, which implied a lot more and cast a much longer and deeper shadow, hadn't provoked a word out of her. Her silence of reluctant acquiescence was enough for him: reluctant, yes, but not disagreeing (the operative phrase being *not disagreeing*). A man who knew to quit when ahead, Don swiftly took leave of the unpleasant topic and became in a hurry for them to part before she changed her mind. "You know, I have a quick meeting. You can wait for me if you want. Please, please, accept this small token from me." He pulled out a wad, offered it to her, but she shook her head and stood up. Then he quickly gave her the itinerary for Sunday: St. Francis Church at nine; family time after church until around four.

#

St. Francis Church, Abay, did not look like a place where sharks came to settle their differences. It was a house for Catholic piety with all the elements of such a place—spire, transepts, altar, prayers and, of course, clergy. The priest had done his best through the poetic sounds and motions of his church service—his grand sign of the cross, the sonorous chant and response between him and congregation, the Latin and English invocations, the blessed hymns of In Perfect Harmony and My Soul Be on Guard ... He had done his part to send parishioners home in pious frame of mind.

Nevertheless, material life started right outside the church, within steps of the church, in the parking lot with the borders of a four-foot brick wall along HM Road, a ten-foot brick wall from the street inward, the portico of the complex for offices and halls, and the church itself. There, in the lot's rectangular expanse of concrete, shiny and shiner cars splashed out. Every model of every year and every class of the Mercedes

105

brand gleamed in open space in extraordinary numbers. Of course, the Rolls Royce, Ferrari, and other rides for the arriviste were on display there as well. Apparently, St. Francis of Assisi himself had decided that being poor hadn't gotten his job done and had rewarded the majority of the members of his church here with an ultimate car in the configuration of SUV, station wagon, sedan or coupe. Internal radar of pride or shame seemed to have guided car owners to where to park. The newer and classier the cars, the closer they were to the purview of parishioners trooping out of the church; the older and less expensive the cars, the farther away in the corners they lurked.

With the latest models and highest classes of cars displayed closest to the church, owners of such cars—people like Mr. Elonowa (Sisyphus), Dr. Ihoeyno, and Don—did not face the challenge of other congregants who had to locate their vehicles amid a sea of metal tops under the grayish overcast of CDKuru. These "blessed families" had the advantage to enter their cars without distraction and drive home with their souls still pure and in communion with their God. But no—they lounged around their cars in the shadow of the church to socialize.

Dr. Ihoeyno and, by extension, his wife stood out; Elizabeth in modest formal wear and the suited Don waited on the sidelines. Dr. Ihoeyno was a tall and heavy man of about "fifty-seven." He had the variegated complexion of someone whose skin had withstood uncountable tubes of lightening creams. At first sight, his face looked like a novice's drawn outline of a face: a straight line down from the skull to the start of the lower cheek, a diagonal line down to the chin, a similar diagonal line up the other lower cheek, and another straight line up to the skull. After the initial impression, however, bulging eyes, a flat-bridged nose with nostrils wide enough to inhale the American quarter coin, and dyed hair filled in the cartoonish outline and gave it a human dimension.

The first and last impression of the wife was that she had an overwrought style. Right away, you saw the vast amounts of money she'd spent on her hair attachments, makeup, and gaudy jewelry adding up to an expenditure that would give some accountants heartburn. You barely noticed her light skin, fiftyish persona, medium size and height, and large clear eyes. She and her husband wore outfits cut from the same gray Guipure lace material. His outfit was a pair of baggy pants, caftan, and overflowing outer garb slit at the sides from the arm to the leg; hers was a baggy long-sleeved blouse with cape, a full-length wrapper skirt and a headscarf that was intricate in design and extravagant enough to fit ten large heads. That the lace material of the couple's outfit was ornate made him look a tad grandiose and made her look grandiose outright.

The Elonowas looked even more grandiose. In fact, judging from attires alone, you could have concluded that Mr. Elonowa's sole prize in the rat race had been a larger cut of the public treasury than the doctor's cut. The stout, potbellied man with charcoal-dark skin had clothed his retinue of seven in black and blue pure Voile lace. He wore a three-piece ensemble. His outer garb was again just too voluminous for his expensive watch to make its own splash, and out came that mannerism of his. Pull the left sleeve over the shoulder; it falls right down. Pull the … The wife and the girls wore headscarves, baggy blouses and billowing full-length skirts. Their spectacle overwhelmed gawkers, and some of them gasped in awe. "Latest," one of them managed to exclaim. "Two hundred US dollars a yard!" Since even a short man like Mr. Elonowa needed about ten yards for the attire—the baggy pants, the caftan, and the long-sleeved, wide-sleeved flowing robe—he had spent a small fortune on this Sunday wear.

The retinues of Dr. Ihoeyno and Mr. Elonowa had congregated in the shadow of the former's tan G Wagon after they seemed to have finished exchanging greetings. Elizabeth stared at the short man. *I wonder whether he remembers me from the crowd in Don's office that day.* He leered, took a step toward the doctor, and hiccoughed to summon all eyes.

"Don't forget what I told you last week," Mr. Elonowa said with a slow smile.

"Public information," Don's father tried to counter, his face grim for a second.

Elizabeth saw it, and her thoughts commented on the two men. *They are agnostics—pure and simple. You can't just step out of church and start pretending to be family friends and then start sniping at each other. Not right here. No church person does that.* Her assessment of the two men had failed to recognize that their conduct agreed with the advice she'd given Gideon once to compartmentalize things so as to survive. In line with that advice, the church was one compartment. Inside it, both men would manifest the Holy Spirit, carry on as if they were pope and bishop. They were most unlikely to snipe at each other or accept bribes inside the church. Outside the church, even a step outside the church, was another compartment. Both men couldn't be holy in this compartment of their lives too. They believed they couldn't survive being holy here. How would they come about the G Wagons, the Guipure lace, the Voile lace, the Brazilian hair extensions …? Outside the church, even an inch outside the church, anything to enable them to "survive" was fair game, including adult sniping in the presence of young family members. And so both men continued to snipe at each other in the shadow of the church.

With a twinkle in his eyes, Mr. Elonowa said, "Sorry but let me know if there is any way I can help you."

"You know I don't need any help," Dr. Ihoeyno said firmly. "In my position, nothing is insurmountable."

"We have to make sure that remains true forever," Mr. Elonowa said and turned suddenly to tell his children, "Say 'Amen!' to what daddy just said." The children chanted "Amen!" without a clue about what they were affirming. The man laughed sarcastically and led his entourage away.

He had won. As Don drove with Elizabeth to his father's house, he was so stumped he initially just kept referring to Mr. Elonowa as "that stupid man" or "that short devil" until he focused his anger to upbraid the man in absentia. "An upstart," Don said at some point. "He used to beg us for deals. Now, nobody knows how he suddenly got money. Nobody! One day, he had nothing to boast about. The next day, he was raining money on people."

She remained quiet until he had spent his fury. Then she asked, "What did the man tell your father last week?"

"You mean that dwarf?"

"Yes, what did he tell your father?"

"He tried to blackmail my dad."

"For what?"

"Dad said it had to do with EC ... EC ... ECO-something."

"Does it have to do with COBD?"

"I really don't know—didn't pursue it."

She started to shake her head in disappointment but stopped abruptly. *Not wanting to know can be a good thing. Ignorance is bliss. That can save somebody a lot of anguish.*

Yet Elizabeth felt the void in his account as she wondered whether the sly exchange at church got Dr. Ihoeyno to explode in rage in his car too. She was concerned about his true reaction to "ECO-something."

# CHAPTER 10

Her concern was whether the issue would affect her, would seep into her mission today. *I know nothing much about Dr. Ihoeyno's character. Yes, I've heard enough whispers to get a key trait of the man. Yes, they say he is Lucifer's own child. Yes, they say he is worse than a serpent. But that doesn't tell me whether the incident at church would foul up his mood at home too and therefore founder my chances of hearing good news about the job. ... Some people just can't let things go—one false step and their response ruins the rest of the journey.*

At home, the family and Elizabeth lounged in the smallest of the Ihoeynos' six sitting rooms after lunch. The family room was as huge as a hall and had a grandiose and regal décor fit for a feudal lord. Nine ornate seats with carved crest rails and red and green fabric called attention to themselves there. They were three pairings of sofa and single seat—each pair on each side of the room—and a loveseat between two single seats on one side. Their bulk would have choked an ordinarily large living room; here, the seats had plenty of space behind them and enough space in front of them to swallow her uncle's two rooms.

The patriarch sat on one sofa, making it the focal seat there. The peeress lounged on the sofa on his right; Don and Elizabeth shared the one on the old man's left. This arrangement had suited Elizabeth's disposition to watch proceedings from the sidelines, from Don's outside shoulder, where she sought to escape his mother's supercilious gaze that made Elizabeth feel like a roach that had just dropped from Mars.

But the old man had invited Elizabeth to his sofa, and she now shared center stage. She sat primly, quite self-conscious about her comportment but observant as well. At such close range, she saw how half-heartedly the man fought nature and how half-hearted his vanities were. He had dyed the thinning hairs on his head very dark but given in to gray hairs sprouting on his hands. He had bleached his face almost ruddy but left his neck to continue to darken. He seemed indecisive about how to tackle the ravages of time on his features, and his wife and his mistress had left him to his idiosyncrasy.

Drinks had been served, and the servant—a slight dark man of about forty—had retreated to hover in the background. Dr. Ihoeyno had been charming, smiling and telling her how beautiful she was, how assured she looked … Perhaps to make her more comfortable, he tried to diminish the impact of the incident at church and joked about it. "The four-footer suffers from the Napoleon Complex. He forgot my name is Napoleon," he said and burst into laughter. Elizabeth visualized a slightly different absurdity: a pygmy puffed out by outsized ego trying to dislodge a heavyweight like Dr. Ihoeyno. She smiled. Don and his mother exchanged puzzled looks. "They don't know I'm funny," the patriarch said. "At least I can now say that someone understands my jokes on Sundays."

Elizabeth asked, "What is EC ... ECO—"

"ECODB. Don told you that. ECODB—that's my term. I should copyright it. But I can bet my last dollar that he couldn't explain it."

"He just didn't try to—"

"That's the problem. He never tries. Easy life, that's all—and his mother keeps making excuses for him."

"Is ECODB related to the CODB in business?"

"I like you more and more," he smiled amusedly. "I see that you really know how to pivot from an uncomfortable topic."

Elizabeth snapped alert. It was one thing for Gideon to read her mind as easily as if she'd confessed her secrets to him; it was entirely something else for this man to know her moves ahead of time. *If this man is a master manipulator as widely whispered, I can easily become his puppet and not know it. Not everybody is like Gideon. Careful now, Elizabeth, be careful with this man.* She said, "MD, what's ECODB?"

"It's Environmental Cost of Doing Business."

"So, it does have to do with that CODB?"

"Yes, it does. It's a simple business practice in an environment full of obstacles. This requires that a gratuity, a gift—a douceur—be given to an executive who clears the way for a transaction."

Elizabeth strained her face to hide her thoughts about what he'd just said. *Oh, bribery! Bribery in the executive suite. Still bribery—just like the policeman's attempted extortion at the checkpoint. ... Yet I must give the devil his due. When I do something wrong I feel it inside. I suffer a ton for it inside. I feel ashamed and less human. But not this man. He simply talked of his bribes as an ordinary thing. Blessed he is with the ability to keep shame at bay. Blessed he is with the power to neutralize the cancer inside that emotion called shame.*

Don interjected, "Dad, why not give him something?"

The old man snapped, "Nobody goes to that trouble for something small. He wants me gone. He wants to move in with his own people. He wants his people in the executive suites so they can siphon millions—not something small, Donald!"

"Sorry," the wife said. "Don't get angry."

"Why won't I get angry?"

"Your doctor said—"

Too late for the doctor's advice, too late for niceties in the presence of a guest—the old man thundered, "Have you asked him how he spent the money from my plots that he sold? First, he sold them for peanuts. Peanuts! Then he burned through the cash in seven days. Seven days! Imagine what will happen if I go abroad for a month and leave him in charge of my deals."

"Sorry," Don and his mother said in unison after the volley. Even Elizabeth felt a little chastised, for the cutting speech, which was loaded with bitterness and reproach, hung over its audience like daggers.

Later, the mood in the room changed. Classical music wafted from a giant TV. The air conditioner hummed quietly. Don immersed himself deeply in drinking his cognac, and his mother dozed. Elizabeth might as well be alone with Dr. Ihoeyno, whose head kept time with the music. She thought that by now he should have told her something about the job—but she'd heard nothing. The gloom of disappointment inched up her spine; still she waited and sat there quietly.

The man excused himself to go upstairs. At this time of the day, the sun was fully stoked, and its suffocating heat laid siege to CDKuru. But the senior servant had anticipated it and had turned the thermostat of the air conditioner way down. Cool or chilly air—depending on one's skin sensitivity—had since settled in the house. The temperature must have been just right for Don, for he too had succumbed to drowsiness. Elizabeth had a different reaction. She felt chilly. Her skin was full of goose pimples, and she ran her palm up and down her arm to warm up.

She didn't notice Dr. Ihoeyno's return until a brown envelope dropped onto her lap. The envelope was jumbo and filled to bursting. She knew right away that the envelope contained money and that the money was—even with the low value of the local currency—still an immense sum.

An old rumor about the man turned cold cash into something else. "Nothing is free—nothing," the man was rumored to have observed. "You have to get to give." Her mind turned the stuffed envelope of money into an envelope stuffed with decomposing rats that leached onto her dress and thighs. *Yuck!* She pulled away from it and it settled on the seat. The impulse to get up and hand the package right back to him seized her. Yet she hesitated, fearful of appearing ungrateful or conceited. A few seconds later, her disgust with the money subsided. She now wished to return it at the right time.

He'd moved away from her to the window. He leaned forward with an air of concentration as if staring through the window at something in the backyard. She waited for him to turn to make eye contact with her. He remained there, in that posture; she felt the appropriate moment to return the money was passing. She took the envelope and tiptoed toward him, mindful of the napping two. When she got close enough to be noticed, she sensed his refusal to turn to her. She realized that nothing engrossed him. He was simply keeping his distance from her and pretending to be busy to make it harder for her to approach him to try to refuse the money.

"Dr. Ihoeyno," Elizabeth whispered as she tried to hand him the envelope, "I can't take this." But he ignored her and continued to gaze out of the window, to remain silent. He seemed to have died standing. She knew he hadn't died upright.

Gravity didn't work that way on earth. Gravity torpedoed the dead. She moved deeper into the angle of his vision. "I won't take this," she whispered louder.

"I give you something small," he said sternly, "you throw a fit. Do you always make things difficult?" The sleeping duo awoke and stared.

She found herself retreating, defending herself: "Oh no! I'm grateful. I'm not trying to make things difficult."

"Then just put the money away."

"I can't, sir," she snapped. Then she recovered from the instinctive chagrin that had sharpened her tongue and modulated her tone. "The money is just too much."

"Don't worry," he said. "I won't go broke because of that."

"That's not what I mean."

"What do you mean?"

Elizabeth recognized the man's maneuver. *He doesn't want us to talk about the main thing I came here for. He knows I didn't come here to collect dole, handouts or whatever. Yet we are only talking about the money in the envelope. I am caught up in resolving an artificial issue. I should tell him that I came here to see if he would reauthorize the job for me—that I didn't come here for money.* However, she kept her mouth shut. The money remained in her hand and her repulsion to the lucre in lieu of a job remained with her as well. Something about the money being in her hand leached her spirit away and dredged up her shame. *I just can't accept it. I just can't accept it. I may have come here to beg for a job, but I haven't come here to beg for money. Won't become an adult dependent.*

The peace in the room had been disturbed. The air

conditioner's hum, faint a minute ago, became quite audible. The room became chilly suddenly for all. "Wale," Dr. Ihoeyno shouted. "Go and turn off the A/C."

Soft footsteps from behind a nearby column faded away from the room. Then the air conditioner fell silent. Dr. Ihoeyno slogged to his seat. Elizabeth followed him. She faced a dilemma after she sat down: The dreadful envelope remained in her hand, yet she couldn't insist on returning it to him in that delicate atmosphere. She decided to wait for another appropriate moment, vowing silently to fight on. Every tactic was fair game in this avowed fight, even leaving the envelope on the chair.

"Wale," the man called again. "You are not doing your job well today. Look at the glasses."

No one really needed the butler. Dr. Ihoeyno himself didn't want any more drinks, nor did his wife and Elizabeth. Only Don wanted more in his cup, but he was willing to serve himself. As he reached for the bottle, he'd said emphatically that he didn't need someone to come all the way from across the room to pour him a drink when he could stretch to do so himself. But neither his father nor Wale would listen.

"I'll just keep the bottle here," Don said after he'd grabbed the cognac bottle and cradled it. "Wale, you can now stop worrying."

Wale grinned, shook his head ruefully and begged to be of service next time. Dr. Ihoeyno rose, called Don "the cognac-drinking egalitarian" and declared it was time for the duo's meeting. This meant Elizabeth and Don would soon leave.

After father and son retired upstairs to the study for a conference of sorts, the wife tried to smooth things over. She toned down her supercilious attitude and got Elizabeth over to share her sofa. The woman was still the second person in charge of the world (her husband was the first), but she had now let go of her whiff of disdain for a commoner suspected of trying to reap where she didn't sow. She began by stating that she'd been married to Napo for about thirty years. "I think I understand him more than anyone else. He is not a bad man. He is really a nice man once you know him." Her light-skinned face dimmed with sorrow as if the world had denied a man who needed understanding his due. Then she permitted a faint smile on her face. "Try to understand," she said.

Elizabeth conceded that the man might be generous but soon found herself protesting that the money was too much to be a gift in CDKuru.

"That's Napo for you," the wife said amicably. She was saying in effect that her husband was too generous and strange at the same time.

Elizabeth's thoughts refused to accept the man as an eccentric. *Seeing him in action today confirmed a few things about him. Your husband is not straightforward. Some people know he's taking bribes, and he just shrugged that off on the church premises. No shame. Nothing. Not even when he talked about it here. Then his pretense so I won't return the money. The end excuses any evil, says Sophocles. What's his end? Why does he try so hard to make me keep the money? No! Your characterization does not fit your husband. If it did, he would have talked about the job. ... It's not kindness when you give somebody money when you can give the person a job—it's a way to ensure servitude.* Elizabeth said nothing.

The woman intoned "Wale" twice. Wale did not rush in. He was a senior house staff—he served the head of the

118

household. So Wale hid nearby and gave no response to the next in command of the house. She bellowed a female name, and another servant hurried in. *This girl should be in school*, thought Elizabeth, the instinctive champion for education.

"Yes, madam," the teenager answered.

"Get me that envelope," said Don's mother. When she took possession of it, she carried on as if the controversy of the gift had been resolved and simply placed the bundle on Elizabeth's lap. There it sat when the two men lumbered into the room. That the son now walked like his father compelled Elizabeth to observe Don closely. Usually he had an easy gait, unlike his father's awkward heavy one. Don's face and shoulders showed more. The long face drooped, and his shoulders sagged.

But after a few anxious moments about him, she turned her attention to the matter of the envelope. She looked for it on her lap. It was no longer there. Her hands were empty; she hadn't absent-mindedly taken it. She concluded that Don's mom must have taken it for a final assault at a later opportune time or that the package had slid down. Whatever the case, Elizabeth felt free of the money. In the car, she decided the envelope was indeed on the sofa or on the floor, for Don's mom, who had walked them to his car, did not bring up the issue again.

#

Don drove north in sullen silence. Traffic was light and he drove fast. In less than twenty minutes, he had emerged from his parents' street, zoomed down three wide tree-lined streets of V Island, crossed the small bridge to the other island, circled the ring road, and entered Oke Bridge—all without saying a word to Elizabeth. She knew he was burdened, but she didn't prod him to unburden himself, didn't ask him what was wrong. *Why should*

119

*I? He is not that young and he ought to grow up.* Don tried to force the action after he entered the causeway: He took the wrong exit. Still she refused to prod him—didn't even ask him why he took the wrong turn. Instead she thought, *If he wants he can take me to Jericho and bring me back to my place. He has petrol in the car. I just won't break the ice for him.* Then he gave in and said, "We need to talk. Let me park at the Lanoitan Theatre."

After he pulled into an empty parking area on one of the side entrances to the mammoth building, he gave her a long bewildered look; she waited him out. "Why do you try to spoil everything?" he asked eventually.

"Don, think a little. You told me he had a job for me—"

"He did!"

"So he finally decides to meet me, but when we meet he doesn't say a single word about the job."

"You have to wait."

"I have been waiting."

"Stop being impatient and wait a little longer."

"Wait till when exactly?"

"Does it matter as long as you get enough money from us to take care of yourself?"

"Yes, it does!"

"Isn't money the reason people work?"

She paused, for the answer at the tip of her tongue was a complicated one. It involved something to the effect that her own earned money would make her feel independent, fulfilled, normal—would fill her with adequate self-esteem and a sense of equilibrium that their money couldn't engender in her. That answer, she thought, would be inappropriate for her audience.

*That will be too tasking for you, Don. You like things simple and easy. My answer has nuance. It's just not right for you.* So she simplified her message and declared, "I want the job more than money from anybody."

"Everybody takes money from us—except you. Why?"

"You are changing the subject," she asserted.

"No, I'm not."

"Okay, how long do I have to wait before he does anything about the job?"

"No worries—you are part of the inner circle now."

"I don't feel it."

"You'll feel it later."

"You and I are already spending too much time together."

He was wounded. "You cringe any time you think of a serious relationship with me," he said meekly. "What is wrong with me that you have to always react like that?"

"Nothing," she said. "Nothing."

The response was sincere and narrow, not diplomatic to assuage his wounded pride. She truly didn't find anything exceptionally wrong with him. He did not have a hideous face, the frame of a gorilla, the odor of a skunk, or the manner of a beast. Besides, he wasn't an idiot, though his mental laziness eroded his brainpower time and again. The one thing that could have raised a red flag had she not been relationship-averse was her dull psychic connection to him, her prosaic feeling for him. Even that didn't mean that something was wrong with him as such. Nobody says that something is wrong with a man just because his girlfriend knows in her soul that her involvement with him would sooner or later be passé. Love is too mystical to

GEORGE O. OTIONO

be within the powers of a man or a woman.

However, Elizabeth's response did not refute or affirm Don's charge that she cringed at the thought of a relationship with him. He must have assumed that the non-answer affirmed his charge, for his manner complained to high heavens of something. He sulked all the way to her house. He didn't even ask, before driving off, when they would see each other again. She didn't care—the affair was supposed to be day-to-day, not something to do with tomorrow or succeeding weeks.

## CHAPTER 11

Two mornings later, on the way to the bus stop, Elizabeth had the handles of her tote bag on the shoulder as she tried to get the bag clamped between her arm and her body to let the thieves on the streets know she wasn't new in town. However, her arm felt an unexpected bulk in the bag, and she became mystified. The urge to know seized her—she halted. But as soon as she did, her thoughts warned her. *People ought to learn to stop indulging their curiosities. Whatever is in the bag will not morph into something else if I wait a little while longer.* She continued to trudge along the dirt track to W Avenue.

She entered a bus for Nihsum, sat squeezed in the Kombi bus, and held her bag onto her body. The bulk inside the bag began to press onto her stomach, and she couldn't avoid it any longer. She slid her hand into the bag toward the bulge, felt it in her palm, and startled herself and the two passengers flanking her. "Sorry," she muttered to them as she thought, *What if someone stole it.* "Conductor," she said loudly to the driver's assistant, who was immersed in his cell phone, "I'm coming down—next bus stop." And when the assistant gave no response, she shouted, "Next stop, conductor!"

And so she came down at the next bus stop, crossed to the other side of the expressway with furtive looks of worry, and hailed a taxi back home. By the time she got home, buried the money inside her clothes in a portmanteau in the inner room and came out to sit in the parlor, she had lost her panic. Then, on the olive-green settee, in the dingy light of noon, Elizabeth made the instinctive decision to keep the money. At this point, she had absolutely no idea why she'd made the decision: All she knew was that she would no longer return the money to Dr. Ihoeyno. Of course, that wouldn't do—not after she'd so recently found the obscene amount repulsive, not after her report to Big Mama about having rejected the "gift." So Elizabeth began to think of the reasons that would justify her sudden decision now to accept the gift. *Too much time has passed. I can't return it now. That would just cause unnecessary trouble. ... Okay! What about this reason? If the Ihoeynos had given me that job I would have earned as much money by now. ... Okay. What about ...* Then she came upon a reason that would wholly benefit her uncle's family, but she tamped down the thought quickly out of fear it might send her to the no-go area of her mind.

Elizabeth faced the old woman not long afterward when she came in and asked, "What brought you home so soon?"

Elizabeth motioned the woman to the inner room, dug out the envelope from the box and piled the money on the bed. A bewildered look came into the old woman's eyes. "What is this?" she asked as if she didn't know it was money.

"They put it in my bag—that's the money from Don's father."

"Put it back in the envelope, put it back in the envelope," she said hastily. As Elizabeth stuffed the envelope with the money, the old woman muttered, "This is just too much. I have never seen so much money in my life. God Almighty! This is more than your uncle's salary for two years."

"I thought so too," Elizabeth said, thinking that the envelope seemed larger now than it was when she first saw it.

"I've lived here long enough to know how things work in CDKuru," Big Mama declared. "He's trying to buy you—you don't need such money."

"Wait!" Elizabeth said as she straightened up to stare into the old woman's eyes. "You are going to keep it."

"Oh no," the woman objected as if frightened. "You have to return it."

"Just wait," Elizabeth insisted.

"What can we do with it?" she asked in an objecting tone.

Elizabeth decided to first try out answers unlikely to make them feel cold. If none worked, then she would have to allude to a recent fear that no one wanted to talk about. But first, delay ill feelings as much as possible. So she argued that the money could be the man's way of atoning for the job that he dangled before her eyes and snatched away. The full body of the old woman's braided hair shook its dissent. Elizabeth argued that returning the money now would be like a death wish. "Don't you want me to get a job?" The braided hair continued its dissenting motion. Suddenly sad, Elizabeth realized she had nothing else to utter but the cold, calculating statement. *I have to be pragmatic now. I have to be the pragmatic one. This family has done so much for me. The least I can do is to help even if Big Mama has other ideas about the money.* So Elizabeth said slowly, "We will keep the money for hospital in case anybody in this house becomes too sick."

She had alluded to the recent deaths of some residents of the neighborhood—residents who had died prematurely because they had nobody to pay for their medical care. Chilly currents ran through the room. Memories of corpses and wailing mourners jangled the nerves. None of the two women could speak or move. In that hush, distant voices and distant sounds reached the room. The continual roar of tires on the nearby overhead freeway, blaring horns, hawkers' voices, music and all filtered in from what seemed a distant world. In that solemn moment, both women cowered before the fear of early deaths and the helplessness of those who couldn't afford medical care at the time the grim reaper was growing addicted to the blood of the poor in Irnopi and beyond.

Big Mama recovered to charge ahead. She took the money, pulled out wads, handed them to Elizabeth and said, "You need some money too."

With that money, Elizabeth did many things. Though it wasn't December, Christmas mood swept her up. She found herself in shop after shop where clothes, shoes, bags and other items called out the names of people dear to her: Big Mama, her children's names, Uncle Barnabas … In addition to the shopping sprees, whenever it became difficult to find a bus, she simply hailed a taxi. When her money started to dwindle, she got more and more from Dr. Ihoeyno. Her drama about the man's stuffed envelope and her protests against accepting it had become part of the forgotten past. Sunday after Sunday, she received a bundle, expressed fitting gratitude to her benefactor who downplayed the whole thing, and hauled the money home.

Sunday after Sunday, she felt less and less that accepting the money ought to induce shame in her, and her unease about it continued to dissipate. Her transformation was no happenstance, no luck of the draw. She'd induced it. She'd inoculated—and thus escaped—the ill feelings about the money by continuously hammering into her head the benign thought that the money was just a gift. *A gift is a gift. A gift is a gift. A gift is a gift.* After hearing that incessantly, she fully expunged from her mind the slimy image that the wads used to have and zeroed in on them solely as clean notes of immense value. And the more she believed her conceit, the more her memory of her past affairs with the Ihoeynos faded until the matter of denied employment and the promised one vanished from her conscious thought. At that point, she became amnesic about her past with the Ihoeynos and her life with them became just all about the present, all about the moment—a day-by-day sort of affair.

Sunday after Sunday, however, the "Welcome home" that Big Mama said to Elizabeth upon her return to their Irnopi rooms sounded fainter and more reticent. In addition, the old woman's actions found other ways to express her displeasure. Not one of the bags, shoes, and clothes bought with the newfound wealth had left the boxes where they were stored. Even when she attended a wedding, she wore her old clothes and shoes and carried an old handbag. Her conduct toward Elizabeth became formal, and they spoke less.

#

Elizabeth ran off to visit Gideon. On arrival at his place, she was coy about the content of her shopping bag when he asked about it. He didn't pursue the matter.

"I have to cook for you today," she declared. They drove off to the market to pick up ingredients for the meals. When they got there, they bought tomatoes, meat, pepper, and onions. So glued and so sweet to each other were they that traders mistook them for a newly married couple on honeymoon. At home, she changed her clothes. She wore his t-shirt and lounge shorts and got to work in the enclosed kitchen. He loitered there, helping any way he could. Elizabeth and Gideon remained besotted to each other until she finished cooking and they began to eat.

While he ran his commentary on her culinary delights, the rice and stew had started to taste bland on her tongue. Worrisome thoughts had dredged a sour taste to her tongue. *When I saw the suit, all I heard was Gideon, Gideon, Gideon. It looked tailor-made for him—I had to buy it for him. Now I'm not sure how he would respond to the gift. ... I can't take it home.* [Stores in CDKuru had no-return policy and she would just have to sell the clothes at a major discount.] *I really wanted him to have it. I've already imagined him several times in that suit.*

After five-thirty, they left for her home in his car. When they got near Proceedings Market, they encountered a batch of passengers on the last leg of their journeys home, passengers getting out of or into cabs, buses and auto-rickshaws. Not here, not anywhere on the route to Irnopi would life go quietly into the night—crowds would swell and teem and buzz as darkness started to creep in, started to dull even more the daily faded hues of the sky.

Gideon drove carefully. Pedestrians crowded onto his lane incessantly, and drivers headed in the opposite direction appropriated half of his lane to convert the entire road from two lanes to three. Vehicles going in his direction managed to move on, albeit slowly. At the bus stop, they stopped altogether. The crowd was larger here and the traffic was in a chaotic deadlock. From their vehicles, several drivers shouted their arguments about their rights of way, horns honked to protest the delay, and everyone else waited to find a way out of the mess. Elizabeth gripped tightly the shopping bag on her lap and said, "Gideon, this is for you."

"What is it?" he asked.

"A gift."

"I know it is a gift. What's inside?" She opened the bag a little; he caught sight of its content and said, "Clothes."

"Suit."

"Where did you get money for that?"

"I told you—"

"When are you going to know that this man is just sucking you in?"

"So you and Big Mama have been talking about me?"

"So she told you the same thing?"

"You are just being jealous."

"Is she being jealous too?"

"She just doesn't like Don."

"Do you even understand what you are doing?"

"Don't you want me to get a job?"

"This man can give you a job in a second—but he just doesn't want to!"

"I have to be patient."

"Believe what you like, but don't try to bribe me."

"Bribe you for what?"

"To make yourself feel better."

"You just don't know what I have to go through because of you."

"You are too blind to see how lucky you are to find someone who loves you back."

"Gideon, our relationship is not meant to be."

"Will you still think that when you get a job?"

"Yes, it is more than that."

"Are you secretly married?"

"No!"

"Should I ask Big Mama?"

"You can ask anybody you like."

"So why are you terrified of being with me?" She said nothing. "I am not married—I've never even been in a serious relationship. Does that change anything?" Her head shook in dissent. "Did a man break your heart before and—" Another dissenting shake of her head. "No more guesswork from me. Tell me why it is so hard for you to accept something right, proper and just natural—something you really want."

Her lips remained sealed.

A bystander sorted out the traffic quandary. He had become the de facto traffic warden, ordering this driver to back up, that one to angle the car the other way … When three lanes of traffic finally formed from the tangle of vehicles, horns tooted to salute the effective knight, and cars resumed their journeys. At Nihsum, twilight hovered over the place, and herds of jam-packed millions of souls bulged deep into the road to sandwich the Honda Civic. Gideon and Elizabeth became claustrophobic. They were so close to the crowd that the elbows of a few short pedestrians jostled whiskers away from grazing the faces of the driver and passenger. They closed the windows and locked the doors from inside. They felt safer.

Suddenly she sighed and said in a low tone full of sorrow, "Gideon, love is not worth it." Her palpable sorrow stunned him, and instinctively he tried to comfort her without impeding her from letting it all out. He remained quiet, drove with one hand, and used the other hand to pat her on the knee area. "My father never got over his lost love. He simply drifted from one thing to another … moved to the village … a PhD holder. … He never recovered."

Gideon tried to prod her to say more. Her mind had

blanked out that forbidden topic. She had never said or thought this much about it before. She focused her thoughts on Gideon's charge that Dr. Ihoeyno just did not want to give her the job.

#

A charge that failed to generate a seismic response from her when Gideon uttered it now started to nag her. It nagged her enough over days that she sought some answers. First, she went to Don to ask why a job that was approved and ready for her would take so long to reapprove. Did they offer it to someone else? His answer was not categorically affirmative or satisfactory: "He hasn't said anything about it to me. You know, Madam Agnes is the middle person on this."

Elizabeth didn't step from Don's office to Madam Agnes's table to continue the inquiry. With people trooping in and out of her office, the place would be a poor location to discuss such a matter. Elizabeth waylaid the secretary in the parking lot the next morning, startling her. "I hope everything is all right," Madam Agnes would exclaim.

"I just want to talk to you before you become busy."

"Oh! We could have gone to the canteen during lunch."

*The canteen isn't suited for this, either,* Elizabeth thought. She said, "I want to know that I will still get the job."

"You will."

"How can I be sure?"

"You don't have to worry about that."

"But how can I be sure?"

"Things are different now. You have stopped running from Don. The doctor will treat you well."

"Treat me well—how?"

"Look, this is not like before, when you didn't care so

131

much for Don."

"You mean when you and Don tried to pretend he has become responsible?" The woman's usual bravado disappeared—suddenly she seemed at a loss and clammed up. Elizabeth realized she had come close to a secret. *Something is going on. All these secrets and lies, and nobody wants to clue me in.* In frustration, she lashed out at the only one of the possible culprits that she could castigate without consequences. "Why am I even wasting my time with a liar like Don?" she asked rhetorically and stalked off.

The plump old woman could be light on her feet in an emergency, and she caught up with Elizabeth in no time, pleading, "Wait—just wait. I will tell you the whole thing." When Elizabeth waited to hear the woman out, Madam Agnes said, "If a woman tells her man everything she knows, even his relatives will become his enemies. You must not tell Don a single word of what you hear from me today." Elizabeth nodded her agreement. "Dr. Ihoeyno has plans for you. Big plans."

"For a job?"

"Yes, yes."

"Why big plans? He can just give me a job."

"Things don't work that way."

"But it did the week I was supposed to escort Don to the canteen."

"Everything is going well—just make sure you don't spoil it."

"Are you sure?"

"Most people in CDKuru will do anything to step into his house—but you are there all the time."

"But why am I there all the time?"

132

"Just wait. Everything has its time."

"Please tell me, Madam Agnes, so I know what to do. Did you cook up something else to help Don look good?"

"Who? Me? I have never cooked anything up."

"Remember, I was supposed to be his steady girlfriend months ago. He told me you came up with that plan."

"I didn't," Madam Agnes said firmly.

"If Don didn't and you didn't, then maybe I'm in something too convoluted for me."

"No! I just didn't tell Don the real plan—I couldn't. The real plan was for him to act as if he has settled down with you so that those girls will stop disturbing him and stop taking his money. Dr. Ihoeyno is really intelligent. The plan has really helped Don."

"So why don't I get the job now?"

"You are not doing poorly yourself," Madam Agnes said. "Things are going to be even better."

#

*Enough is enough,* Elizabeth decided in rage that she'd made the inquiry at all. Henceforth, she would not tell Gideon anything about her dealings with Dr. Ihoeyno. All Gideon had done with such information was to use it to challenge her thinking and fill her mind with doubts and suspicions about the man's motives. *He doesn't understand some things. Gideon just doesn't understand some things. The hope of getting a job from the man helped me carry on with my life. It gave me something to look forward to. Instead, Gideon kept analyzing the situation and stampeded me into asking when I'd get the job. So what that I've learned that the whole thing is twisted? Does that give me hope? No! Does that give me anything to look forward to? No!*

133

So Elizabeth's retreat from job hunting ended. She had to scrub her experiences in that endeavor out of her mind. This was no time to remember the past gargantuan obstacles to meeting officials with the clout to hire, the dead ends at every turn, the miseries that became a wound in the heart, the infinite losses of hope that leached off all the stamina to keep going … She had to clear her mind of each aspect of those horrible experiences and push herself to begin her active job search again.

Her daily haunts were no-brainers, for no areas of CDKuru fired the fantasies of the unemployed more than the business districts of Sogal Island and V Island. The central bank, commercial banks, investment banks, national companies, multinational companies, international organizations or entities, and even state agencies had their marquee offices towering in both islands. Every morning, she dressed in fitting business clothes and left home early to go from office to office in search of that one-in-a-million official who could and would work a miracle for her. Her handbag was slightly heavy with copies of her resume and her mind full of impressive points about her candidacy.

After bypassing the ubiquitous series of guards to get into the offices proper, she usually found a sympathetic employee to direct her to who could help. No matter the cutthroat reputation of CDKuru, it still had, in low stations, a few people who saw Elizabeth's doe-eyed innocence and just wanted to help her. But the creatures in the executive floors had a different disposition. "Come back next month," some of them glibly offered. They really didn't want to see her now or in the future once they realized her mission—they just wanted to extricate themselves from her ambush. If they saw her shadow next month, they would veer to the opposite direction. They knew this when they mouthed the words; she knew it.

Some executives who were willing to see her in the future would ask, "How much do you have?" Then they would quote her an inordinate bribe for the job. The trouble here was that she had not heard of or seen anyone gamble money for a job and won—very many of the jobless had already lost borrowed fortunes to such hustlers. She did not want to join the queue of the duped.

Some executives asked her if she could land a big customer for their banks. She understood the imputation of that question: Could she be a siren and get a sugar daddy to use his influence to steer a company account to their bank? Well, if she had the temperament for an affair with a sugar daddy, she wouldn't be this hard-pressed for a job. One executive befuddled her by having her visit him week after week after week but then ended up telling her she wasn't really serious about the job. What did she do? she'd asked in alarm. The answer: "You know what you didn't do." That door slammed shut in her face.

## CHAPTER 12

She persevered—she had no choice. She kept looking for one benefactor, just one. She continued to wait in the lobby or in the executive office suites for the right ear and continued to ride elevators or walk stairs up and down looking for someone who knew someone else who knew … who could hire her.

Gradually her mind began to fill up with the bitter thoughts that she had scrubbed off recently, and she began to sense an encroaching emptiness. She numbed herself against it by convincing herself that someday, perhaps when she least expected it, she would find the job—she numbed herself by giving her hope no timeline and letting it float indefinitely into the future. She would get the job someday, she told herself. And she persisted by leaving her home every morning and trying her luck in every office that allowed her in. The physical exhaustion of trekking from building to building in humid heat, of climbing stairs in high rises, of standing a lot in lobbies, and of indefinite waiting in offices helped her in one way. It cured her intermittent sleeplessness, and she slept much better in that house.

Later, however, the job search became sporadic, and Elizabeth drifted back to Dr. Ihoeyno. Not everyone supported that. Gideon, who was visiting her, did not, and he ended up pushing her into an area of her psyche she had always avoided. "This whole thing is murky," he had said. "Sometimes it looks like an excuse to be around your friend."

Elizabeth flared up: "First of all, I don't need an excuse to see Don. Second, you are a major part of my problem. I have told you—I don't want to be in love!"

"Again, why did you invite me out?"

"I didn't know this would happen. I thought that you were just an ordinary person … that we can just talk and socialize—"

"Okay, what if your father suffered—how do you know you will lose me?"

"A million things can take you away—a car accident, sudden illness—"

"My God! If we think like that, the whole world will grind to a halt."

"You still can't deny they are possible."

"Their opposites are all possible too."

"Yes, they are but I don't want to take a chance to find out."

"There has to be something more to this," he said. That cut deeply into her, and she froze. "You have never said a word about the woman at the heart of this—your mother."

Currents of chills began to flow up and down her insides. She felt like she was on the verge of catching a cold. And she kept shivering. "Let's not talk about this anymore," she said.

"We can't," Gideon said gently. "If your hang-up about love dooms our relationship, I have to know the details of it. I am not prepared to walk away from you with a vague notion of why you are on this self-destructive course."

"I have no hang-up and I'm not self-destructive," she said quietly. Then she whispered, "She died."

"How old were you when she died?"

"Does it matter? She died!" She had shouted and had become misty-eyed.

"Sorry," he said.

"What kind of person are you?" she asked rhetorically in a quivering voice. "To keep pushing me to talk about something horrible."

"Sorry, but we can't keep avoiding it."

#

If Gideon was against Elizabeth's association with the Ihoeynos, her uncle was wholeheartedly for it. He had met Don one Saturday afternoon and had become richer with a gift of half his yearly salary and had seen a vision of the Promised Land. "If only God will make him marry Elizabeth," the uncle had hoped aloud. Unfortunately, he had said it to the wrong audience.

"The way you talk sometimes," the wife said as she got up in a huff to leave him.

"Show me one person who likes suffering," he countered.

She stopped moving and turned toward him to say, "Your wife must like suffering."

"I can't even have one opinion because I am poor."

"When you talk, just remember you are poor."

"All right, let's start praying that Elizabeth finds a poor farmer to marry."

Big Mama came out of the encounter with her husband with a clear sense of what she must do. She must distance herself from the web that had caught her husband and Elizabeth.

She did so on Monday morning, after Elizabeth had piled up money on the bed for safekeeping. Instead of carting the money away to a safe location, Big Mama surveyed the scene with a cross expression on her face. "You brought the money," she said eventually. "You keep it." That episode jarred out

Elizabeth's old misgivings about the money, and she began to feel censured and ashamed anytime she saw or imagined she saw a severe look on the old woman's face. The woman's face had become Elizabeth's conscience. It started to make her feel disgusted with herself—to make her feel as if a part of her had rotted and she couldn't pull it out. Her spirit sank. Her entire being shrunk. She started to avert her eyes from the face and to feel like slinking off into hiding. That they lived in such tight quarters and crossed paths too many times meant she had nowhere there to hide. She felt besieged—she began to abscond from the house during the day to drift aimlessly around town.

Eventually, without a dime of her sudden wealth, she went on a noontime trip to a place she had avoided for some time. A pilgrim of sorts, she contended with the inconveniences of her journey without a moment's quibble. While being squeezed on both sides by two fat women in a crowded bus, she had the grace to smile continually at the infant that one of the women had placed right in front of Elizabeth, who had to sit ramrod straight to keep from squishing the child. While being jostled in semi-crowded bus stops or suntanned in the course of trekking between bus stops, she remained cheerful. When the record *I Got You Babe* blared at the Proceedings Bus Stop, she hummed along, emphasizing the stanza about love not paying the rent—clearly tweaking herself. She had not been this light-hearted in a long time.

At her destination Elizabeth stood dwarfed by the mountainous compound wall of the block of flats. The car and pedestrian gates were locked. Reflexively she banged on the pedestrian gate. It opened halfway. She remained rooted there—couldn't move any feet. As if she'd been sleepwalking since and had just awakened, she felt the dawning sensation that she was actually in front of Gideon's flat. Self-doubts beset her. *How is he going to receive me? How will I initiate conversation? Will he throw me out? Or is it better for me to turn back now?*

Better or not, she found herself moving again and her hand pushing the steel gate. It creaked fully open. She crossed the threshold, saw his car parked on the concrete courtyard, and trudged to the staircase in the middle of the three-story building. She began to climb the stairs.

At that moment Elizabeth failed to recognize she inhabited two different worlds, one foot here and the other one over there—failed to know she was betwixt and between. On one hand, she had become a part of the Ihoeynos and had kept letting herself be drawn toward the epicenter of their den; on the other hand, she had come to her sanctuary with pure motive, had followed her heart to this place. She was a woman at the mercy of two opposing forces trying to claim her. Her terrors within had commingled with her desperate drive for the job to continually pull her away from her endearing feeling for Gideon, yet a force inside her continued to impel her toward him.

She was ringing the bell of his flat. It rang too long before she was let in. "Did I wake you up?" she asked, taking the seat near the door.

"No," he muttered and volunteered no explanation for the delayed response to the ringing of the doorbell.

"I was beginning to think that someone picked you up. ... You didn't answer the bell. ... You are not talking. Are you angry?"

"I couldn't come to the door right away."

"Are you mad at me but not mad enough to tell me?" He

ignored the question. She reached for the handle of her bag and got up. "Should I leave? ... I better leave—I don't want to waste your precious time."

"I'll tell you when you start wasting my time."

She stood still, handbag dangling from her shoulder, and examined him. He wore a beige cotton tunic atop baggy gray pants and black open-toed sandals. But the tunic's three buttons were undone, the sandals unbuckled. "Oh! I see you were getting ready to go out."

He gazed at her for a few moments and then thought for a few more. She knew he was trying to determine what to do with her. No! Not that he was rethinking his decision not to throw her out of his house. Yes, he was disappointed in her, but not enough to want her out of there. He was considering whether to ask her to come along to his destination. She already had the answer for the yet-to-be asked question. *That's a yes! I will go. Wherever. Even to hell. Yes! Yes! Yes!*

That resounding yes in her mind was born of two parents: her subliminal guilt about her absence from him and the blissful power of his presence. She realized how much she missed him and sighed. *I wish we could just sit down in this living room until the end of the world. Just the two of us. Just be together here—like this.* But that was just the delirium of love twisting her thoughts briefly, for she knew they were leaving the house very soon.

"I finally got the location of a man I have been looking for in a long time. They say he is different from my mother's other relatives. He is blunt. ... This is it. Whatever he tells me today will end my inquiry about what my mother did."

Gideon and Elizabeth left for the Iyedaf address of the

man. They joined the moving traffic on O Expressway, turned onto I Road freeway, and drove down one side of Iyedaf to the J underpass turnabout to double back to the other side of Iyedaf. They turned off the freeway onto a crowded narrow street full of potholes and began wading through the herd of pedestrians who only parted at the last minute for the car to inch along. When Gideon had managed the drive for about half a mile, looking along the way for the two landmarks of a bar and three shops on a three-story building, he parked the car as near as possible to the open gutter so that other cars could squeeze through without shrinking the width of his car.

They came down to the street sounds of a chattering crowd and music from shops. She followed him. They stepped over a grimy gutter filled to the brim with all types of stinking trash and entered the building.

The building had grimy walls, dilapidated air of utmost neglect, and cramped space for a maze of corridors. A zigzag of steps led to rows of single rooms facing each other across the narrow, shadowy corridors. Burnt or broken or age-discolored bulbs dangling overhead could not take advantage of the rare supply of electricity to illuminate the corridors. Gideon and Elizabeth stopped to adjust their eyes to the twilight before he led her to an open door on the ground floor. He knocked several times before an old woman parted the curtain to answer him. "I am looking for Mr. Uneuko," Gideon said after initial greetings.

"How does he look?" the woman asked.

"They say he has very, very heavy lips," he said.

"Ah!" she exclaimed. "To each his own—to him his lips. Check upstairs on top of this room."

Yet when Gideon and Elizabeth entered the room

143

upstairs, they found not a man with thick lips, but one with wispy lips. Their quarry had moved, and his old room now belonged to someone else. They had to find their man. Outside, as Elizabeth waited in the car, Gideon pressed his cell phone into service until he came up with a pseudo-address on a sheet of paper. And off they went—they joined the freeway back to the O Expressway, turned onto it, passed the exit to Gideon's place, and continued toward Elnugeja.

The rain had come suddenly and heavily, pouring down as if an invisible dam in the sky had broken. Rain claimed a lane or two in different stretches of the road. Jaywalkers on the freeway ran helter-skelter. A few cars were wrecked in the commotion that resulted from the abrupt onset of the torrential rainfall, and the engines of some cars had sputtered dead in the course of wading through floods on the road or thereafter. Gideon and Elizabeth only had to deal with damp clothes and damp skin after zapping shut the car windows. He handed her a hanky. He chuckled and thanked her when she dabbed him with the hanky after she had dabbed herself dry with it. Then they continued to peer intently to see through the continual gauze of waterfall on the windshield and beyond as the drone of the rain and the whimpering of the strained windshield wiper filled up the car. He needed to avoid both waterlogged trenches on that slick road and pedestrians darting across the freeway.

They got to Sogal/B Road, turned left, and stayed on the expressway until they reached Urus Bus Stop and turned right. Traffic had come to a crawl and the flood level on the lanes seemed to have risen. Once they entered the mouth of the so-called City of Fortune, the mouth of JA City, they came face-to-face with the panoply of that rain there. The flood was stationary and high enough to float a boat. As a matter of ingenuity, an enterprising boy had fished out a canoe and ferried people through at a charge. Roofs of submerged cars poked out. Hardened residents took off as much of their clothing as decency allowed before wading through the belly-high brown water that sat on the road. Others were paralyzed in cars, in buses, under the eaves of shops, or under the pelting rain—they knew not what to do about that brown small river on Ijedeyo Street.

Elizabeth imagined the same scene replaying on the other side of the flood—people, especially those with their own transportation, being quarantined there inside their cars and moping at a flood that would take days to subside. "What if we had been trapped on the other side?"

He laughed aloud, then said, "Your imagination is on the tragic side."

"No, but what if we had been trapped there?"

"We would have found a hotel there."

She relaxed.

#

Upon return a few days later, they found the flood subsided to a manageable level. Pedestrians were no longer intimidated by the flood—they crossed it without a moment's hesitation, though they had to stop first to roll trousers up to the knees, hold up skirts and wrappers above the knees, and take off shoes, socks, and slippers before wading through with their footwear in hand. Motorists too continued on to their destinations, though at a much slower pace. They had only one lane open for traffic both ways—the other lane remained buried under a high flood that crested and shimmered above the hoods of a few trapped cars. Two Good Samaritans ensured that traffic moved at least. They shouted and signaled directions to each other as they synchronized their control of motorists from opposite directions through the open lane. One hand stopped traffic on one side; another hand waved on drivers on the other side. These impromptu traffic wardens soon became rewarded with tips from motorists.

Gideon inched the car along the submerged road, pushing more water toward pedestrians but not with enough force to splash the water on them. In the flood, Gideon and Elizabeth had turned left onto Ugaeze Street and had hung onto the safe lane for about a block. Thereafter, cars began to crawl on two lanes. The street was a very busy thoroughfare, a seedy place where cheap joints selling all types of food and drinks and all sorts of merchandise jostled an infinite number of street vendors and hawkers for space. The buzz of overcrowding and deafening music from some joints and CD/DVD street vendors mixed in the air. The majority of the crowd just loitered; just a fraction seemed to have a destination. People danced on the street to the competing music in the air, and the rowdy crowd commandeered the lanes of the road. Cars honked to find a way to squeeze through.

"These people have it backwards," Elizabeth shouted to Gideon above the cacophonies from stores that seemed to dot every building on the street.

Though he concentrated on inching his way through this multitude of mortals, he replied, "Welcome to the jungle."

A jungle, indeed! Human tangle was dense in the extreme here. Gideon saw no lane to follow amid the masses occupying the front of buildings and the street proper as if they owned the spaces. Each time he seemed to have room to inch along, the herds closed up the trail again from all directions like ants that had suddenly lost the trails of their leaders and so scampered blindly about. Gideon crawled on without seeing an inch of the road—the car seemed to nudge people out of its way.

Gideon and Elizabeth got to Nadolo without their car pushing anyone down, but then they had to contend with a sodden, sordid narrow trail that ended at a clogged canal. The trail itself, which lay under rubbish, puddles and mud, was flanked on both sides by squalid structures of plywood plastered with wet carpets of all the riotous colors of this world—all of the carpets threadbare and faded. The car had started to sink once it turned into the alley. Elizabeth knew this was the end of the road. Gideon himself seemed to have felt so as well, for he had immediately thrown the car into reverse to back out. He found his car stuck, tires spinning frantically and digging holes. He rocked the car forward and backward several times before he could back out of there. After he parked, he sat in the car in a pensive mood for some time before he looked up to see the road ahead. She remained quiet.

The windows of the car remained closed, yet they couldn't escape the boisterousness of the living from outside. Teenagers and young adults playing soccer on the alley were howling taunts at each other and whooping with joy. Their bare feet were encased in mud and their bare chests glistened with sweat as they played in that improvised field with rubbish heaps as goal posts. A gaggle of spectators shouted directions and commentaries. Above all that, the radio voice of an almost naked child provided a play-by-play announcement of the game to an audience that clapped and cheered his virtuosity as much as they did an extraordinary dribble or pass.

147

For a second Elizabeth thought that Gideon had gotten caught up in the game, but she realized he'd been studying the trail when he nodded toward it to say, "I should not have brought you to this place."

"Don't worry," she said with bravado. "I can manage."

"There is no easy way to the last house on the left," he said.

He was right. After they came down and took a few steps toward the house, they jumped backward. They had done so instinctively to retreat to safe, solid earth because they had felt the wet ground sinking under their feet. The ground under their soles had been shifting, threatening to cave in on them. The uncertainty about whether the next step on that porous soil would suck them down into a subterranean cesspool had frightened them. They were exchanging bewildered looks when they heard an encouraging voice tell them, "Don't worry. You will get used to it." Though they thanked the man who had spoken to them, they still didn't move. Then he said, "Just look at the boys playing in it."

That alleviated Gideon's fears, and he took two steps and waited for Elizabeth to join him. She, too, saw the man's logic: If these boys—many of them her size—could run around and throw their weights around on that trail without falling through to an underworld, surely her weight couldn't be enough to cause the ground under her to buckle despite its shifting sensation. She joined Gideon. But they had to stop again. This time, the problem was how to proceed in the face of deep mud and heaps of rubbish. The man came to their rescue again. After he ascertained their destination, he directed them to follow the path of rubbish on the left. They saw at once what they hadn't seen before—the heaps of rubbish on the left served as the bridge to the houses on the left.

## CHAPTER 13

They got on the pedestrian bridge fashioned from mounds of trash. With every step, their feet sank into the quagmire, making it squish and send up rotten smells. Elizabeth came as close as ever to levitating, with her torso held upward and her legs on tiptoes. Flitting toward her destination, she balanced her weight on this toe, that toe. She had unwittingly found her gift to be an aerialist. But Gideon was so concerned about her safety that he, himself, nearly had a misstep that would have sent him tumbling into the muck and the oozing filth. "Are you all right?" he shouted.

"I will be … when you stop worrying about me and concentrate on your steps."

They passed the boys playing soccer in the mud and arrived at a fully waterlogged portion of the trail. Here, the flood from the clogged canal at the end of the alley had breached a makeshift levee to submerge the front of the last three houses on both sides of the trail; here, the flood was just about an inch lower than the already elevated door thresholds of these houses. So when one of the soccer players waded in the water to retrieve their ball, the flood continually galloped, threatening to crash into the houses. Elizabeth was so mesmerized by this continual close call, by this precarious cohabitation of the flood and the houses, that she stopped moving. After the boy waded out of the flood and the seeming danger to the houses passed, she inched along again, perching here and there on any solid items she could find on the ground.

They finally reached the last house on the left. The canal

had come into full view. Boxed in by rows of dilapidated residential structures, it was a cesspool choking with all manner of garbage and overgrown with algae. The algae were so thick in some parts they shrouded the cesspool underneath completely. Rank odor of rotten and rotting matter and the stench of mold poisoned the atmosphere. Gideon and Elizabeth ducked quickly into the house. But the smell didn't fully go away. Inside the room where they finally faced the man Gideon had vowed would be the last window into the circumstances of his mysterious origin, the odor hung heavy and everywhere. They had to bear it—they couldn't turn back now.

The room was gloomy, humid, and miniature. Although the man's tiny wife stood with one foot in the room and one outside, she still seemed to hover over Gideon and Elizabeth, who sat squeezed on a tiny bench. An arms-length across from them, the man—tall and of emaciated features--squeezed onto a jerry-built bed (more crib-sized than twin-sized), propping himself against the wall. He had been coughing intermittently since they came in. He'd been told their mission, but he had continued to cough without responding. "Sorry," Gideon said eventually while trying to maneuver himself up from the seat. "I didn't know you were sick. We should come back when you feel better."

"I'm not dead yet," the man said in a quivering voice. "I can still talk."

Gideon stopped trying to get up and waited. Again the man remained silent. His silence dragged on until it began to wear on both Elizabeth and the man's wife. The former unconsciously clasped her hands; the latter tapped her foot on the floor as her hand continually clutched and released the door curtain nervously. Gideon sat still and stared at the man. Suddenly the man muttered as if he meant to address himself, "The One who created us made sure to leave us a mystery."

He paused, pulled himself up a little and sighed. "I believe your mother died not knowing the answer to a tormenting question. Did she conceive you before she met and married your father or not? That's the question that clutched to her throat. She was afraid of getting the wrong answer. So she would mope a lot and lose herself. … Why was she always sick? Now we know why. She was suffering from something that nobody else knew about. She suffered it to her grave. … Your father is suffering now. Look at me: I am suffering it too." At this point, his voice rose as his tone grew stern. "But look at you—they gave you so much education, gave you all this good life. You could have been a farmer's son loafing around in the village. Look, out of the suffering of other people, you became a winner. Accept that advantage and stop chasing shadows."

He curled up on the bed and turned his back to the guests in an unmistakable pose of dismissal. A ghostly hush permeated the room. Not a single thing or person stirred. In time, both Gideon and Elizabeth would find themselves near their car, with the eerie silence and the man's wife at their heels. "Things are not always what they seem," said the old woman. "Fate intrudes and what can we do?" She was crying. Elizabeth too began to cry as she pleaded with the woman to stop crying. Gideon's eyes moistened too, though he said nothing. He had brought out his wallet and emptied its content onto the woman's hands. Elizabeth had done the same and rummaged inside her bag for every stray penny she could find for the woman.

#

Rainy season had set in. Day and night, the saturated clouds over CDKuru let loose sheets of translucent water over the city, sometimes for a few hours straight, other times for as long as eleven hours. Floods ran amok in the city: They swallowed roads and gutters, buckled homes, inundated buildings (some losing nearly the entire ground floor), and massed into Olympic-sized pools in many areas. Unemployed muscular men in these areas suddenly found themselves straining to keep up with the demand for their labors. Their customers were well-dressed male and female strangers to or from work or business. Each needed to get past the pools without drowning or making a fool of himself or herself and so had to pay a brawny man for a piggy-ride, for an over-the-shoulder-carry or for a spot on an overcrowded makeshift canoe to cross to the other side.

The heavy rainfalls brought benefits too. CDKurienes without need to venture out of their homes and those who had no trouble with floods in their homes appreciated the noticeable drop in temperature. Elizabeth had been enjoying the weather at home despite the occasional inconvenience of hailing taxis in the rain and venturing out on waterlogged roads. She sweated much less than usual. On nights of heavy rain, she relaxed even more, with her mind lazily following the sound of downpour on tin roof, with her mind lazily following the lullaby of rain.

The sedative effect of the rain on Elizabeth had been possible because of her state of mind, her internal temperature. Had her psyche been disturbed and out of balance, she would not have cared at all about the cadence of rain on roofs nor would it have been lulling her to sleep. For the first time in years, she was enjoying a rare peace of mind, the peace of the innocent. The essence of the words that the crying woman had uttered about

Gideon's plight and its concomitant victims had resonated in other fateful situations. Elizabeth now saw ill fate as a tyrant. *It decrees how its victims' lives play out, assigns them burdens to carry to the grave. ... Look at me—no, no, no! Look at another unfortunate group. ... Say, the descendants of a known monster. They are liable for things outside their control, for things that fate decreed. Fate chose their genes, chose the barbarian to be their forebear. Yet they have to go through life feeling some guilt for what fate had set up for them. ... Fate was worse than the world's worst tyrants all put together.*

"Things are not always what they seem. Fate intrudes and what can we do?" Elizabeth had recited those truisms in her mind, recited them under the drones of the rain, recited them in the cool aftermath, recited them in the middle of the night and at any other solitary time. And with each recitation, she found her thoughts keening to the logic of those words until her mind filled up with the idea she was just an instrument of ill fate. Destiny had used her at her purest and most innocent moment to do its dirty work. Destiny … She stopped that trail of thought. She stopped herself from delving into her own case of fate's intrusion. She had skimmed the idea and again evaded introspection.

Gideon prodded her. "My search has ended," he had said. "But we have to address your own issue."

"I have no issue," she said.

"Face it—you have a hang-up."

"No, I do not!"

"How old were you when your mother died?"

"I won't talk about that!"

"How did she die?"

155

"Does it matter? She died!"

"How?"

Elizabeth refused to answer.

"How?" he persisted.

"She was killed."

"Sorry. I didn't know. Sorry."

#

The rainy season had tapered off. Heat had returned with vengeance. Floods were receding to let roads and gutters to poke out again. Mud, debris, and decay stood out again on the streets. With time, the floods dried out, saturated gullies and potholes dried out, and gutters again bore the thickest stew of decaying trash and the steadfast stench of uncountable rotten smells all at once. By now, the panoply of unremitting rain—its drama, shocking visuals, and concrete damages—had fully given way to the diffused and less dramatic appurtenances of the heat. Excluding those scarred from losing someone or property to the floods, CDKurienes were already too enveloped and preoccupied by humid heat to find their minds drifting to the past rainfalls and their tyranny.

Now Elizabeth could go out anytime without worrying about floods soaking her or quarantining her far from home. Not only did she take advantage of this situation, she did so often—in fact, she left home too frequently. The daily egress allowed her to lose herself in the crowds and hustle and bustle of the city and, in doing so, escape anyone who could provoke her thoughts of her mother's death. Elizabeth left home at an opportune time in the morning and returned when all the other occupants of the household had come home, knowing that to stay home and mope around at the wrong time would have set off Big Mama's inquiring tongue. The girl was determined to block out that memory that Gideon had brought fleetingly to her mind.

By night, however, Elizabeth found she hadn't done enough. Though no one could remind her of the burden at such times, her mind itself would not let her be. It would rev and try to make sense of the whispers and sentence fragments about her mother that Elizabeth had overheard over the years; she would pull her mind away from making that dreadful inward journey and will herself to escape into any thoughts incapable of spiking or sinking her heart rate. Her mind would spin away from that to the more urgent thoughts, to burning thoughts of some event better buried in the past; she would will herself to dwell on the details of her pitch-dark milieu. Back to her mother the mind would spin—and the loop would start anew.

So, around and around Elizabeth's mind would go without resting long enough on any thoughts until she dozed off from exhaustion—only to wake up from the catnap to succumb anew to the tug of war between what her mind wanted to think about and what she felt she could handle, between the past and the present.

That the nightly occurrence made it clear that rarely can a person outrun himself or herself failed to get into her skull. Each dawn she heaved a sigh of relief that the city had opened up so she could escape the intimations of her dreadful memory, so she could flee from her past. One evening, after her usual flight from the house during the day, she had returned a second before nightfall. She couldn't have timed it better again, for everyone was home and getting ready to sleep. Big Mama could not say much to Elizabeth, though the old woman wore a deep frown. "Don't tell me again that it is too late to eat," she managed to grumble.

"Sorry," Elizabeth said. "It is too late for me to eat."

"This has to stop," Big Mama warned darkly.

Elizabeth knew the warning was about the food and her vanishing acts. The city had begun to shut down for the night. The day's nonstop din of engine drones and tire swishes on W Avenue gave way to the night's occasional tire roars on that expressway, the coming and going on the corridor of the compound ceased, and the entrance door of the house was bolted. Big Mama uncharacteristically stayed put in the "parlor" as the young ones locked its door, lifted the center table onto the settee to create space for their sleeping mat, spread the mat on the floor, and lay down.

She blew out the lamp, set it atop the fridge (with a box of matches near it), and sighed into the other room. The lamp there went out too, and blindfolding darkness interred both rooms. Nothing happened for a long time, nothing—except the quietude of night descending on CDKuru. Elizabeth, wide-awake in bed, had her mind following this distinct deepening of silence and inertia.

Though she was alone on the bed, she curled up as if someone else crowded her there. Time seemed not to pass, which made the night stretch out like an eternity. Suddenly she was ashamed. Her stomach soured. Her body flushed hot. Life drained out of her as never before, drained out until she felt like a carcass losing bodily fluids and shrinking. She could have sworn that a million eerie voices booed her inside her head. Elizabeth sought to escape the experience immediately and forced herself to think of something—anything not tragic. She began to think of Big Mama's assertion that profound despair became manageable with time. *Big Mama is right! Big Mama is right! The woman is right. I can see the difference between how I felt immediately after they took the job away from me and how I feel about it today. At the time, my wound was fresh, my pain raw and too much to bear. ... I had no hope. I felt so shattered that I believed my life had nose-dived, that I couldn't survive another day. Gloom was burying me alive. But now, I don't feel it as horribly as I did then. Not at all.*

As usual, with the fan motionless because of another power failure, humid heat threatened to roast every flesh in the rooms, and sweat oozed out of Elizabeth's upper body, soaking her wrapper, pillow and bed. In the past, she would turn away in search of a dry patch on the bed or fold the wet part of her wrapper away from her body; tonight she lay still on the soaked bedding—her skin hardly reacting to the usual clammy sensations of soaked bedding that you would have thought she had grafted leather on her skin. In the past, the mosquito or mosquitoes buzzed into her ears, forcing her to swat at random at where she thought she'd heard the buzz last and ending up slapping herself time and time again on the neck and face; tonight she lay still, indifferent to the sibilant noise of mosquitoes and the deoxygenated air in the room.

Elizabeth had escaped her problem for just a few minutes, but that was it. Using a less unpleasant thought to overcome her shame didn't mean she'd flushed it to the depths of the ocean. No. The shame sloshed around inside her with such force that thoughts of the tragic cause of the shame—the repressed tragedy itself—loomed at the margins of her mind. Cold sweat began to pour out of her body and she started to shiver. Fear, the icy hand on the soul, had caused that and much more. Her sweat glands had turned cold. Blood in her veins had turned icy. Her bones had frozen. She trembled as well, well aware that trying to escape the horror made her feel that way—but terror, sheer terror, paralyzed her. Her guard against the dreaded thought remained up as she shuddered and shuddered with fear until she became a wreck on her bed.

#

Big Mama sat in the dingy room that morning without moving a muscle in a long time. Though she wore her work clothes—denim gown, rubber slippers, and headscarf—she had apparently decided to defer her domestic duties. Normally, she did them as soon as her children left for school so that she didn't have to jockey with the other homemakers in the compound for space in the kitchenette area. Today she would have to jostle with them later for a spot for her kerosene stove and for enough space to wash clothes and utensils. Now she had to wait. And she had the look of a person ready to wait for an eternity. Her sight was trained on the bed in the "parlor." Elizabeth, who'd actually dozed off earlier in the morning after her uncle and the children left the house but had since woken up to find herself a quarry, pretended to be asleep. That didn't budge the old woman.

"Good morning, Big Mama," she said eventually.

"Good morning," the old woman replied. She got up, went to the door to pull its curtain back and returned to her seat. Faded sunlight arced into the room. "Have you finished sleeping?"

"Yes, I have."

"Now you can tell me what has been chasing you away from your house these days."

Elizabeth had prepared an answer but hadn't expected

160

the line of questioning to be without preamble, hadn't expected a cannonball so soon. Thus, she needed a few moments to untie her tongue before she said with as much conviction as she could muster, "I needed to be alone."

"Oh!" said Big Mama in an incredulous tone. "You needed to be alone."

"Yes."

"Certain people are called adults for a reason. They have enough sense to know the obvious. It's obvious that you wanted to be alone. Why? Why do you suddenly want to be alone?"

"My mind has filled up—I need a break."

"A break here and there is not bad; it is even very good. It lets us detox, lets us refresh ourselves, and let's us see things better. But beware. Sometimes people say they are taking a break when they are trying to run away from problems."

"I am not running from anything."

"Just beware. Running can only get you so much time. The problem will still be there to tug at the heart."

Elizabeth said nothing. Big Mama stood up, took a few steps toward the inner room, stopped for a contemplative second, and returned to her seat. She reported that Don had visited a couple of times. He had also left a cell phone and the message: "Call me on it or leave it on so I can reach you. You can return it later if you don't want it."

"When did he leave the phone?" Elizabeth asked.

"More than a week ago."

"You should have told me earlier."

"Do you want me to get you the phone now?"

"No," said Elizabeth.

"That's why I wasn't in a hurry to tell you. Besides, I

could only tell you in private. Your uncle has been talking about how lucky we are that you met such a rich family. He will almost commit suicide if he hears you have been avoiding that man."

"Big Mama," Elizabeth said. "Don is not bad. Nothing is really bad about him. He tries for me, and he can be nice. He could have been responsible also. Sometimes I blame his parents for letting their money to spoil him. He's really not bad as such. Big Mama, why don't you like him?"

"Elizabeth," Big Mama said, "liking him is something for you to decide. That's not a question for anyone else. But you better be sure you know what you are getting into."

"Do you like him at all?"

"I am not looking for a boyfriend or a husband."

Elizabeth sat up on the bed. She had on a loose purple negligee and a black nightcap over her hair. Her legs swayed idly several times, bumped against the coffee table, and returned to the board of the bed to cool the heels. Her fingers tapped nervously on her lap as she waited for Big Mama to continue her reports. But the old woman refused to go on. Eventually, Elizabeth could wait no longer. "Did anyone else visit?" she asked.

"What do you think?"

"I won't see him again," Elizabeth announced as her eyes blazed with fury. "He won't stop telling me what I don't want to hear."

"Things like what?"

"Things … things I just don't want to hear."

"Did you tell him—"

"Yes, I told him—"

"Did you tell him you won't see him again?"

"He is intelligent. He will realize that easily."

The old woman stood up, shook her head in frustration, and left for the kitchenette area to attend to her chores.

# CHAPTER 14

Elizabeth continued her routine of leaving home before the civilized visiting hours of the morning and returning just in time for bed; both men continued to meet her absence. One day, however, this fleeing of her house left a vacuum from which sprang the personal demon she'd been trying to outrun. That morning Big Mama was being gracious to Gideon on his third fruitless visit—offering him refreshments, apologies on Elizabeth's behalf, and encouragement to feel at home—when the old woman added something else. "Don't take to heart some of the things that Elizabeth does," she said. "She's trying to come to terms with herself."

Gideon saw an opening. "Who killed her mother?" he inquired.

"Who told you Elizabeth's mother was killed?"

"Was she not killed?"

"But who told you that?" Big Mama asked.

"She did."

The woman paused and lost herself in thought. Then she said, "There are things I can tell you; others I won't. ... Her father and mother were studying at the university when they married. Their life together was set—he was a lecturer with a few months of school left before his job became permanent and she became pregnant. That's when trouble started: We started hearing 'no jobs,' 'no jobs,' 'no jobs'; started hearing that even many people with jobs would lose them. ... The crisis that we've had now for more than twenty-five years had started. Her father could no longer get the job. He couldn't find another job either—

nobody could find a job. It was because he had no job that the tragedy struck." She fell silent.

"What happened?" he asked.

"What will happen is that you will hear the rest from her," she said emphatically. "It's her life, her puzzle to unravel. We can prod her, but she has to do it herself."

When Elizabeth returned and heard the report of the discussion, she was annoyed. She saw it as an intrusion into her psyche. *They do not know what I have to go through! They can talk and talk—do they feel my anguish? And Gideon—that Gideon!* Not only was she angry that Gideon had been at it again, prodding and prodding, she had caught a whiff of admonishment in Big Mama's tone during the report.

In the dead of night, Elizabeth found herself remembering against her will the day gritty reality smashed into her delusion of supplanting her mother with her caregiver. She was ten then, and up till that age, no adult had directly or indirectly addressed her with either the matter or the manner of her mother's death; all Elizabeth knew of the issue had come from overheard whispers or from snippets of hushed conversations that left sentence fragments in mid-air when she unexpectedly came upon people talking about her. Her knowledge of the death, therefore, had the quality of a rumor, which allowed her to suspend the matter from her mind and shroud herself with the belief that she was born by the woman who'd nurtured her ever since she could remember. Elizabeth even called the lady "mother," and the woman as well as Elizabeth's father had sort of gone along with the illusion. But that had to end because the lady, her maternal relative, needed to get married. Duty had already made her reject three suitors,

166

which left her poised for life-long spinsterhood, when a fourth man came for her hand. Every altruistic person (Elizabeth's father especially) welcomed the opportunity with great joy.

"I have to get married," the lady had told Elizabeth between tears as both held on to each other. "I have to go away from here."

Elizabeth had succumbed to the burgeoning grief of maternal love found and lost, sobbing along with the woman. Eventually she managed to ask, "Why don't you marry my father?"

The woman had stopped crying. She untangled herself and stared at Elizabeth in surprise. "Your father can't marry anyone," she said. "He blames himself for your mother's death."

"But he didn't kill her," the child persisted.

"We all know that," the woman said. "But in life people sometimes feel guilty for something they shouldn't—yet that burden weighs them down."

That was the first time (at the age of ten) that the undertow of subliminal horror from her mother's death had affected Elizabeth. She had felt the chilling sensation at the core of her trauma—willful in the extreme—cut its way to the surface. She had shivered into the warm arms of her caregiver then.

Tonight, the cold came back. Ice inhabited her veins, and she broke out in chills the size of pebbles.

#

That was it. Elizabeth blamed Gideon for provoking that memory and decided to cross the Rubicon to let him know this was farewell. She reminded herself of the great advantage of a skin-deep relationship—how it left heartaches, vulnerabilities and traumas out of the equation; how it left one blasé and the soul unbothered, untouched at the core that mattered the most. One didn't cry a river when an unloved partner moved on—one privately said, "Good riddance." Elizabeth fell in with Don's camp. Most of her entire time away from home—away from home because she was avoiding Gideon—she spent hiding in Don's place. While he was at work, she would be there reading and watching television—activities she hadn't enjoyed since her arrival in CDKuru. She also made sure that the male servant did not keep ordering the female cook to do his job and that the girl actually had time to cook. On occasion too, Elizabeth went out with Don before returning home late. To Don's infinite joy, he had heard his father speak in glowing terms about how the romantic pair benefited each other very well. Yes, Don had gained a few pounds since this arrangement began and, on her account, had deprived himself of the nightclub scene more times than he would have liked, but these paled into insignificance beside his wish for the father to believe that the son had outgrown his frivolousness. Don could cite the affair now as proof he had devoted himself to a respectable girl. As for Elizabeth, she spared not a second worrying about how involved and serious the whole thing seemed.

The lone thing of note for her during this period occurred on the Saturday afternoon both of them went to an eatery for baked chicken, pies, and drinks. They were sitting, awaiting their orders, when her memory stirred and she recognized a man she thought she had seen time and again among the crowds of that city—a stranger's face that looked familiar. In the late thirties, the man had the bland features and the retreating manner of a person born to remain incognito even in public. His trade tool, however, betrayed his anonymity. The camera, roped around his wrist and half-buried in his caftan, had caught Elizabeth's eye and triggered her memory. *I've seen this man at one restaurant before. I think he's photographing us. But why? Why would anybody need our pictures? Who would need our pictures? ... Maybe I'm mistaken about the man. Maybe I'm imagining things.* She decided to ignore the man with the camera. Nothing else before the incident or after stood out for her during the escapades. She basically did things for or with Don and didn't have to worry about Gideon.

Then came the Sunday. That Sunday, after the usual family rendezvous at his parents' home, Don zoomed from V Island to Ajeki as if the devil were after him. Conditions were favorable to his design to get to his house as soon as possible. CDKuru had emptied out for holidays, and Don—as well as the other drivers still in the city—had open roads (freeways indeed) to ply. He was also practically solitary in his car. In just the first few miles of the drive, Elizabeth had succumbed to the cool comfort of the air-conditioned car and to the smooth rhythms and euphony of steady speed that lulled her to sleep ten minutes into the journey. Don had kept his speed gauge fluttering far in the right side until he got off the third mainland bridge. Traffic was slightly more on I Road, and his perceptible drop in speed roused Elizabeth from sleep.

"We are already here?" she asked in surprise.

"Yes," he mumbled. Lanes were free in front, but he couldn't get to them. A car ahead of him and another on the right lane had boxed him in. Both cars maintained a similar tame speed, forcing him to tag along when the open road yonder beckoned him. He tooted his horn and honked, but the drivers did not budge. "Why won't the fool get off the speed lane?"

"What's the hurry?" she asked. She sat up, fully awake now. When she got no reply, she turned to inspect him. He was brooding. "What's bothering you?" she asked him.

"Nothing," he said and laughed nervously.

She watched him drive a short distance and knew he was lying. He'd started to honk again. This time his driving became slightly reckless. He veered right as if he must squeeze his car into the right lane, swerved back to his own lane when the white Peugeot refused to let up, and repeated the sequence—his car zigzagging. In the course of this, he startled Elizabeth out of her wits when his car, inches from her seat, seemed destined to smash into the other car.

"Stop this now," she shouted. "You can't be driving like this."

He did stop. However, she was sure now that something had gone awry. Until then she'd never, not once, seen Don drive like that. In fact, he usually complained about "drivers' madness here." He'd say "here" with a dissociating spin as if he were merely visiting CDKuru, as if the city were a way station for him. She gave him a searching look. *What's wrong with him now? What can it be? ... Did something happen in his father's study before we left?... The man is tough and gets on people's nerves. But a rich man has certain liberties—one of them is to make his son quite capable of misplaced anger.*

Indeed, her suspicion was on point. Don's mood was fouled even before he found his car's access to the open lanes temporarily denied. From his father's study, Don had borne in mind an order much taller than he was. He knew he'd been set up to fail, but his weakness, his fragile will, stopped him from refusing the assignment. Ironically or strategically, when the old man assigned it, he'd skewered the son for being weak and, after softening him, challenged him to prove he was a strong man.

Elizabeth and Don arrived at his semi-detached home and let themselves into the living room on the ground floor. The room, spacious enough for a small crowd to spread out to jollify, had an entertainment wall unit that stretched out spectacularly between the door and the bar to display an 80-inch flat screen television with giant speakers and a sound system better suited to disc jockeys. The maid and the butler had vanished, but the generator, the lights, and the air conditioner were on—apparently on for a very long time given the biting cold air in the place. Elizabeth was shivering. "Please turn off the A/C," she said. He did. He also opened the window as well as the door, though he pulled shut the door's wrought iron barricade. Blazing heat from outside later made the place hospitable enough for Elizabeth to sit without shivering and fighting off chills with arms clamped across her bosom.

The television, left on too by the household staff, was flashing fast images of music videos and blaring sound. Don turned it off too. Then he got ready for his test to prove his mettle as a strong man. He took off his jacket, laid it on the loveseat, and sat down. He sat like a man at ease with himself. His body splayed across the seat, one arm draped over the back of the seat and the other arm draped over the armrest. A line from Shakespeare flitted through her mind. *Why, then, the world's mine oyster, which I with sword will open.* Nevertheless, the cocksure attitude did not keep a set of his fingers from tapping nervously. She sat primly on the sofa to his right, expectant.

\#

The sun continued its inexorable descent in the sky. In a few hours, it would get below the horizon and darkness would reclaim CDKuru. For now, the star emitting light and heat from the center of the solar system positioned itself where the two in the living room could see it. At this time on a Sunday too, almost everyone was home getting mentally ready or resting for the workweek ahead. Generators were at peak service and their cacophonies in the vicinity or farther away reached Elizabeth and Don as background noise.

"You see," he began. "We can't just keep doing this."

Mystified, she waited for him to continue. But he dawdled on in silence. His eyes evaded her gaze, slinking away to stare at a corner as he stalled to be prompted. His fingers couldn't keep still. She waited. Seconds ticked by—yet she heard nothing else from him. His silence started to irritate her. Suddenly, being forthright became a virtue to Elizabeth. She imagined Gideon in such a situation. *He would have already told me what he had in mind—he would not stall or sound cryptic or become suddenly tongue-tied. No!* She glared at Don to continue.

"You and me," he said finally.

"Stop beating about the bush."

"You know what I'm talking about."

"No, I don't," she said firmly.

"Well ..."

"Just say it," she enunciated.

"It's not easy," he protested.

"Just say it!"

"My father wants me to marry you," he said softly.

"Your father wants you to marry me," she said in a tone

of reproach.

"I want to marry you too," he said quickly. "You know that."

An uneasy silence overcame them. Elizabeth began to think and think of her quandary. Eventually she got so introspective that her mind's eye saw her situation as a pictorial unspooling like a silent horror movie. She saw her lifelike replica perching on the precipice of a foggy ravine, getting ready for the plunge, but tarrying because she couldn't see what lay at the bottom, couldn't tell whether she would land on fine sand or on jagged rocks. Nonetheless, she slipped and started tumbling down.

A cold fever of fear flushed through Elizabeth. She shook herself out of that nightmare, looked up slowly and squinted a few times to clear her blurry vision of introspection. However, for a second she saw the living room blanched by light—Don and his appliances and his furniture all submerged by a flood of milky light—as if the fog in her mind's eye had suddenly flooded her location and swallowed her. She blinked a few more times before her eyes cleared.

"Why did you wait for your dad to say it?" she blurted.

"I would have. You never gave me the chance."

"Did I give you the chance today?"

"What do you mean?"

"Did you get a different behavior from me today that made it easier for you to say what you just said or did he make you say it?"

"Of course not!" he shouted, sitting up in a huff.

Elizabeth knew that the idea of succumbing to his father's pressure had mildly irritated Don, that it cast him as a full-grown weakling and dependent, but she couldn't change course because she needed to know what had motivated this big development in their relationship. "Okay," she said, "why did he say you should marry me?"

"Look, he has his faults," Don said amicably, before declaring: "But no one is going to tell me why I should marry you."

"So, he only said 'You and Elizabeth should get married'?"

"No. He said I was under your control." Don allowed himself a wry smile that tried to underscore the insanity of his father's statement. "He said I've got to prove I'm a strong man and set a date for the families to get together."

"Why do you want to marry me?"

"I'm fond of you."

"You are fond of many women."

"That's not fair."

"So, why do you want to marry me?"

"You don't think I'm educated enough for you?"

"Don't try to evade my question—you want to marry me. Why?"

"If that guy asked you to marry him, would you ask him why?"

"You see, you don't even know why you should marry me." He said nothing. She stared into space in thought, feeling pity for him. *All right, so the tyrant decreed it and the son panicked along only to act cool now. So what? He wasn't trying to lie to me; he was trying to tell himself something that will make him not feel bad about himself. ... He was just shouting to himself and to the world something to help him with his human dignity. ... Yes, as my father told me, sometimes people need dreams, fantasies, delusions, and lies to keep going. Don needs something too. He's human.* Then she said quietly, "I'm not sure about getting married."

"You know I'm okay with our relationship, but now—"

"But now your father is involved," she interjected with sarcasm that quieted him. Then she muttered, "Why didn't you express yourself for once?"

"There was no point in getting him angry."

"So, what do we do now?"

"Talk to your people."

"Just like that? Do I even look like someone who should be getting married? Do I—" She stopped herself from crying out about the unsettling fate of a jobless educated woman being stampeded into marriage. She asked, "What happened to the job he was supposed to give me?"

"First things first," he urged.

"You mean last things first?"

"He likes you very much; he will take care of you."

"I don't want anybody to take care of me. I just want a job."

"You can take care of yourself in other ways too," he said. "A job is not the only answer."

"Don, all that I hope for is for a job."

"No one in CDKuru ticks because of a job—people tick here because they are loaded."

"I will tick because of a job."

"Don't you understand that you are getting more money from him now than you can make in a job?"

"Whatever I make will be enough."

175

"Why do you always make things difficult?" he said heatedly.

"Why is he not giving me the job?"

"You know he's hurrying us because of you?"

"Me?"

"Yes, you."

"What did I do?"

"You fight everything."

"Like what?"

"Like just disappearing for no reason."

"I can only blame myself for this. I would not have been here to listen to this talk of marriage if I had really disappeared." She had stood up, bag in hand. She was fully composed and fully aware of her quagmire. *I've been in this now for more than eight months without advancing an inch toward my goal—if I continue this discussion with him for the next eighty years, I will still not advance an inch toward getting a job from his father.* "Bye," she said without rancor or heat.

Though he called out to her to wait, she didn't. When she got out of the compound, she stopped a cab and went home.

#

The proposal sobered Elizabeth up. She couldn't be in limbo anymore. From now on, she couldn't just escape her demons by burying herself in Don's world when it suited her; she had to either stay with him till death parted them or leave him alone. Now she had to make a choice—a real choice.

# CHAPTER 15

The next morning Elizabeth left home in a midi shirtdress and shoes that she'd bought with money from Don's father. The dress, gray and linen, had loose three-quarter sleeves, two front pockets and a belt. The shoes, classy black wedges, and the nice clothes distinguished her enough on W Avenue that a taxi ignored hailing "poor" passengers for Elizabeth, whose nice outfit made her look like someone who could pay well—for in CDKuru if you don't look it, don't bother. She got in. Solemn as the bereaved, she arrived at the offices of Dr. Ihoeyno to have an overdue discussion with him.

The ease with which she had her audience with the man underscored her importance and value to him. In the reception hall filled with all sorts of hustlers and overcrowded as a bazaar, employees with the uncanny sense of picking out anybody of value to Dr. Ihoeyno had rescued her from the gaggle jousting to get in to see the man. One of the employees had escorted her out of the place to the office of the secretary to the managing director. Elizabeth sat there and began to watch a large flat screen television beaming world news. Almost immediately, a tray of cold drinks and biscuits appeared on her side table. Another employee had delivered the refreshments. He wore a dress shirt, a tie, and an ingratiating smile. He said, "Madam, this is for you. If you want, I can get some very good things from the management canteen. Do you want the menu?"

"No, thank you," Elizabeth said. "This is enough."

The secretary supervised the proceedings from her seat. Rumors and whispers about the woman had coalesced into voices in the air around Elizabeth. The voices kept whispering, "That's Dr. Ihoeyno's mistress. That's Dr. Ihoeyno's mistress." She was about fifty, light-skinned and rather well proportioned for her age. The designer of her green Mikado skirt suit would have been proud of how the split neckline top with lapels and a closed button accentuated her flat belly and her restrained chest. Her makeup affected a simple and casual style—an esthetic she'd picked up when she lived in Paris at a steep cost to her paramour. You barely noticed the makeup on her oval face or the craft that gave her thick black hair of medium length a swept-back Bob style, but you saw her casual chic. She knew she had je ne sais quoi, though she said nothing of the kind to Elizabeth.

"You are lucky you do not have to work to trap Don," the secretary said after the man left. Then she took a veiled shot at her rival as she made her main point: "You do not have to fake a pregnancy like some people. Yet you walked out on him—you have to tell us 'yes!'"

The speed of news of her response to yesterday's proposal startled Elizabeth, who mumbled something incoherent. She thought that nibbling at her biscuits and sipping her drink would save her from delving into the matter, but found them tasteless now. "Do you know when I can see Dr. Ihoeyno?"

"Finish your refreshment."

"I have finished."

"Let's go then," the woman said. She led the way in a catwalk. Elizabeth followed the woman out of the large office to a private corridor and into Dr. Ihoeyno's office suite. Huge double doors opened, closed and Elizabeth was alone, lost in an office with very high ceiling, massive velvet drapes (now pulled back), giant glass windows tinted blue and views of the island.

178

She had stopped walking to orient herself to the unexpected sight and space that were as spectacular as they were vast.

"Over here," Don's father called out, smiling. He was in a lounge area of chunky furniture—an area with a Persian rug, a center table flanked by several brown leather armchairs and the lone oversized wingback chair of flowery fabrics and tufted buttons and brass nail-head accents in screaming displays. He was sitting on this chair, which stood in front of a wall full of his family pictures. He wore gray pinstripe suit, white starched shirt, and navy blue tie and shoes.

"First time in my office," he said amicably. "The proposal should have come sooner to get you here sooner."

She waited until she had sat down on an armchair before responding, "You know I can't consider that when I don't have a job."

"I am a hardened old man. You can tell me—you have a different reason for being reluctant to marry Don." When she said nothing, he asked, "Is it because you are in love with that other boy?"

"No, it is not that."

"What is it then?"

No answer jumped up and down with fervor in her mind. None. No answer jumped out at her. All she knew was that every part of her told her not to marry Don, not to marry Don. Why? Only God, only Allah, only deities on land and sea, only … knew the answer. But she couldn't say that to the old man. She reached for that canned idea that people frequently used to wiggle out of marriage proposals. "Dr. Ihoeyno," she said slowly, "but what if I don't like him enough?"

"You are the right woman for him."

"You won't worry if your son is marrying someone who doesn't like him enough?"

"My grandparents did not marry because they liked each other enough. My parents did not marry because they liked each other enough."

"But that was in the old days."

"Look, technology has not created a new emotion for a man and a woman. I did not marry in the old days—still I did not like Martha enough when we married. She had to pretend she was pregnant; I had to marry her. But look at us today. She is one person who will remain with me even if I suddenly lose all my money."

"I won't want Don having a mistress if I married him."

If that was a veiled shot at the old man, it didn't hit him, for he said, "Loyalty is all that counts."

"I will be loyal to you even if I'm not married to Don."

"I need someone in the family," he said with a sad face. "I need someone in my family. Look at Don. Just because I put in his name three plots that shouldn't be traced to me he thought they were his, and before I knew it, he auctioned them off. Three choice plots in V Island for peanuts! Imagine that! Should I rely on him to take charge when I am not available?" The man had scowled and shaken his head incredulously at the memory before he returned to his present quagmire. "I won't be like one former MD who keeps crawling back here for small deals because he didn't stockpile enough money when he had the opportunity."

"You are a very rich man, Dr. Ihoeyno."

"I can't leave enough wealth for your grandchildren if I'm booted out in a few years and if I don't make money on all fronts now."

She realized that the man had deftly steered the discussion away from the topic that brought her here. *I didn't leave my house to come all the way here to talk about the marriage proposal—that was his idea, his topic. My issue is different.* She asked, "So, what about the job?"

"You will get a job," he said. "But you will work for me."

"You mean in this office?" she asked dubiously.

"No, in my own company. You'll be in charge."

"I didn't know you had a company."

"I've always worked with people informally to do deals on my behalf. Now is the time to formalize the whole thing. I'll make the most money with a company." He brought out a document from a file and showed it to her. Her mouth opened and shut in astonishment. Mrs. Elizabeth Ihoeyno was majority shareholder and CEO of a company. He began to chuckle.

"I … I have no experience for such a position," she said eventually.

"You are the only one I trust for the job."

"But I won't be able to do it."

"We have legal and accounting firms behind you. Besides, I would still be orchestrating the whole thing. Don't worry."

"CEO?"

"You'll just be the face of the company. Stop worrying."

"So when am I supposed to start this?"

"As far as I'm concerned, as soon as possible. Right now, this company has the big project to build an estate of flats, duplexes, and homes for employees. Our company will get the contract and sell it to a contractor."

"That will be too much for me."

"I know you can sign papers. That's all you will do."

"Please, just give me a regular job here."

"Then who can do this for me? Who can I trust to do it for me?"

"Please," she pleaded. "Your old way has worked for you."

"You understand accounting. What's a twenty-five percent cut when you can make sixty? You are not the only person who needs something. I need something too."

"I can't be a front for a company."

"Stop trying to make this look bad. Nobody is going to be a front—we are talking about a business."

She begged him. "Please let somebody else do it."

"She who fights and runs away lives to fight another day," he said in dismissal. "When you see that my plan benefits both of us, come back and we'll plan the wedding."

#

Elizabeth went home and told Big Mama everything—everything she, Elizabeth, knew about the grand scheme to get her to marry the son so that she could front the father's company. The old woman listened with a frown of concentration as the young one's account of her last two days began, took shape and concluded. Then Big Mama began to listen to her own thoughts. She sighed eventually. "I can't tell you to marry him or not to marry him," she said. "But if the dead can commit suicide, your dead father will kill himself if you do what that man wants you to do."

"I won't do it," Elizabeth said.

"You better not."

"I've already told him."

"Are you going to tell Gideon all this?"

"No."

"Why not?"

"I don't want to."

"Why not?"

"I have enough problems. I don't need a troublemaker."

"What exactly has he done?"

"He tells me things I don't want to hear."

"Things like what?"

"Things that are of no benefit to me."

"Like what?"

The tones of both women had been sharpening as the old one needled and the young one waffled. Now both were angry: Elizabeth sullen and refusing to answer; Big Mama glaring for an answer. As their impasse drew out, the old woman exclaimed, "Someday, you will vomit that poison that's causing all this."

Elizabeth fumed silently.

By the next day, however, the two women had tabled their sore topic because of Elizabeth's all-out search for a job. Now that she knew Dr. Ihoeyno's position, she marshaled all her resources to hunt for employment exactly as she'd done before Don's promise of a job—only now she did so in well-tailored business attires that favored her enterprise. She pressed the hunt as if she had nothing to fall back on. "You have some money," Big Mama said. "Take the attitude of a long distance runner. Pace yourself and be patient for the long haul."

"Thank you," Elizabeth said in a quiet tone that conveyed her heartfelt gratitude.

Elizabeth had wandered this wilderness enough times to

183

know how to get to her quarry. Once she got to any office gates, she cast off her humble attitude and affected a haughty one. She would stride into the premises with the uncommon poise and condescending air that important guests there displayed. And like them, she would remain in her own world past the guards as if they were there only for lesser mortals. If a guard was reckless enough to bother her with the question of whom she'd come to see, she wouldn't break her stride while allowing the first name of an executive to escape her lips; if a surname had to be had, she added over her shoulder, *Oh, Mr. So-and-so.*

The impact of a girl being on a first name basis with a male executive rarely failed to be decisive, though. This was because gatemen had learned from experience that they were apparently expected to be clairvoyants: They had to anticipate the executives' every wish for every visitor. If a useless guest came to the office, he or she had to be discerned as such and hounded off the premises at once. If a young wild thing in a supposedly hushed affair with a boss pranced through the gate, leaving scandalized gawkers behind, she ought to be left utterly alone—no due diligence needed here. The last thing the lowly employee at the gate would do was to get the name of that boss out of the girl's mouth by asking her whom she was there to see. Otherwise, the gateman would consider himself lucky to just be summoned, berated and confounded with the shouted question: "Do you want the whole world to know that that girl was here to see me?"

At the oil parastatal in V Island, Elizabeth had come to see the deputy managing director—though Mr. Owarab did not expect her any more than he expected the thousand others who had one favor or another to ask of him. She knew she couldn't

184

have his audience if she headed straight to his office to jockey among the crowd inside his office lobby to get past his personal secretary and other staff. So Elizabeth planted herself near a strategic but obscure door at the back of the parastatal's skyscraper. Senior management solely used this entrance. She waited in a shadow, her eyes monitoring a special zone of the parking lot.

The skyscraper of nine floors had less than two acres of potholed parking lot. Space was premium. By eight-thirty that morning, cars had already filled up the lot for all comers and spilled out into nearby streets; only the few reserved spots on a fenced-off zone remained vacant. Intermittently, an official car parked there, and a senior executive emerged. Then, around nine-twenty, Mr. Owarab arrived. A corpulent man in his late fifties, he was average in height and light of complexion. He had an arched waist that gave him a stooped posture. His hair was thick and overgrown and could have been a mini-Afro had age not given part of his pate a permanent clean shave. Though his eyes were blood-shot and rheumy, they caught Elizabeth's fetching sight parked near the door and shone with recognition.

"Good morning, Mr. Owarab," she greeted as she stepped toward the man clad in tan caftan and green sandals.

"Don't be so formal," he said genially and then chuckled at what seemed a lost cause. "Just call me 'Uncle T.'"

"I have to talk to you," she said earnestly.

"Okay! I thought perhaps you got lucky."

"No," she said softly.

They climbed the steps of the building to a guarded corridor, and he led with a propulsive gait and the gingerly steps of a man with acute waist pain. Elizabeth followed at a measured

185

pace, cautious not to bump into him and tip him over. The corridor led to a reserved elevator. Once Elizabeth and Mr. Owarab stepped into the elevator, he dismissed the elevator operator from his post and closed the door. The ride had just started when he said abruptly, "I don't like ceremonies. We can talk here."

Her spirit sank. *When they are in a hurry like this ... He wants to discuss my employment in an elevator. ... right here. Oh, no! Oh, no!* Her energy leaked out. Suddenly weak, she propped herself on the wall and held on to a rail. "I have to have a job," she said in a nervous voice.

"I can get you a job. No problem," he said. The tone was factual. Then he advised her with a sly smile: "Don't be childish. You have to help your case. You don't expect to come in here and just get a job for free. Things don't work that way."

The words needled into her and she tensed herself to curtail the sting. Finally he restated an old requirement: "But it's up to you. If you want, we can go somewhere now."

That odious requirement of going with him to a hotel room got her again. It hit her solar plexus with the power of a sledgehammer. She grew weaker, so weak she slumped against the wall. The two needed to say nothing more to each other. Each knew the other's position. The elevator reached the ninth floor, tarried for a second, and hurtled down. It jarred her on landing—she left there with a dazed look of defeat.

She shook that off and charged ahead. But, after running into one obstacle after another, she began to hear the voices of self-doubt grow more ardent in her head. *I can't get a job. There's no way I can get a job.* This was when she went to bed one night and found herself unable to escape Mr. Owarab in a nightmare.

Both of them had been in front of a desolate hospital, where she cowered before him. His facial features kept transmogrifying. One second, the nose grew too big; next second, the forehead became too large ... Yet she recognized him in the various guises as his face continued to transform and bear down on her. At a point she leaped off, got suspended in the air, and still frightened, sensed herself dropping slowly into his claw-like hands.

Elizabeth's conscious sensations at this point cut through the nightmare, for toxins and bacteria had so coated her tongue that the foul state of her mouth overwhelmed everything else and she startled awake.

Thereafter her spirit started to grind down with each step she took in her job search. Despair started to eat her up again. She became a zombie again. She trundled out a few more times before a corrosive belief of never finding a job claimed her soul.

#

Idleness and circular thoughts of anguish had forced Elizabeth into a peculiar relationship with time. Nights dawned into days and days dusked into nights and on and on the pattern repeated itself until the usual distinctive features of passing time faded off. Though the cacophony of stereo music that blared in the compound from morning to evening on Saturdays and Sundays ceased on weekdays, the rowdy announcement of weekends wasn't enough to help her date the passage of time, for one week was just like the other. During this suspension of time in her existence or even thereafter, Elizabeth couldn't say with certainty how long she'd sequestered herself in her Irnopi compound.

"Take it easy," the old woman adjured. "Misery won't solve the problem."

But those words frittered away from Elizabeth. Her sorrow had become a force onto itself and she sorrowed over every aspect of her fruitless job odyssey. She sorrowed over the loop of hope and despair … over her few real prospects of getting a job. Yes, that especially! Being tantalized, having a job within grasp, wounded the soul most, cut deepest into the soul. She sorrowed that in her elevator meeting with Mr. Owarab she had been so near yet so far. That conundrum left her feeling so cheated and robbed and wounded in her soul she grew deaf to the old woman's mollifying words.

"Stop worrying," Big Mama said. "Go and see Gideon."

Elizabeth sat home in her trauma of misery. Once, just once, she wondered if she was her own worst enemy, if she'd unwittingly ruined herself with a fantasy. In other words, was the unique, tranquil feeling of pure choice, of deep affinity with someone else, of love—Petite's "pie in the sky"—subconsciously at play here? Was that really why she didn't accede to Don's proposal? Was her conviction that she needed a job before marrying him merely a smokescreen, which had now turned her opportunity to get ahead into something vile and venal? Her moment of wonder flitted on without affecting her mood. So she remained crushed and sat there zombie-like until she was practically dressed and pushed out of the house by the old woman, who said, "Go out! Go wherever you want. But go out before you kill yourself in this house."

## CHAPTER 16

Elizabeth visited Gideon twice to inform him of her situation. On her first visit, she found the information clutched to her throat like a dry cough. She sat in his presence in his living room trying to lubricate the parched throat with her saliva until she eventually said she had come just to see him. He sat impassive on the opposite side without comment as his eyes pierced through her. She suspected he knew the purpose of her visit but was refusing to help her broach her uneasy topic, refusing to prod her. He was primed to wait for her to—on her own—hack out what lodged in her mind.

On the second visit, both sat where they'd set their buttocks during the last occasion—face-to-face across an invisible barrier. They sat in silence. He kept his eyes on her; she averted hers. The prattle from the compound guard's radio and the occasional motorcycle or car horn sounded fainter and fainter as silence in the room deepened into eerie solitude. She bore her uneasiness for a while, fearing he would reproach her once she uttered her news. Then she hiccoughed in a nervous attempt to get on with her task. "You know what I have come to tell you," she began and paused. Silence enveloped the room again. She burst out, "He asked me to marry him."

His response was cynical: "Why am I not surprised?"

"Is that all you can say?"

"I can say more and worse."

"That's typical of you. I expected you to blame me and make me feel bad—"

"Don't try to—"

"If you'll let me finish … I couldn't tell you right away because I was afraid of all this."

"To what do I owe the honor of hearing your secrets again?"

"Your attitude made me stop telling you about them."

"The attitude didn't change—so, again, why were you in a hurry to tell me this?"

"Because I thought—fine! Sorry I told you."

"You and your games and lies."

Her eyes flashed with anger. "Which lie have I told you?"

"You told me your mother was killed."

"She was."

"She died because your father didn't have a job to take care of what he needed to take care of."

"You are so righteous you won't understand."

"Your father didn't suffer for lost love—his problem was guilt."

"If he hadn't cared so much for her, he would not have felt so guilty that he destroyed himself."

"Is it guilt that's destroying you too?"

"Please, please, stop this!" She was on the verge of tears but succeeded in keeping her eyes dry. He stopped. "What I have been through since I met you is just enough. I've had horrible thoughts. My mind going the wrong places. Things I had been able to forget have come back to bother me."

"Why don't you see a psych—?"

"Why don't you leave so I won't have to marry him?"

"I've already left. I mean, I haven't tried to see you in weeks."

She suddenly began to implore him. "You don't visit your ... your father. You act like you have no parent here. You have nothing here—just go back to where you came from."

"I have to finish my project."

"You can't even start it."

"I have—the last two weeks."

"Please just go back. You don't belong here."

"I may not belong with you but I belong wherever I choose."

"Please don't push me into marrying him."

"Is that it? Am I keeping you from getting married?"

"You are pushing me to get married to him!"

"Fraud yet again. I hope they know this sham marriage is because you are trying to hide from me."

"Don't worry. I won't have a sham marriage. Besides, his father knows about you and doesn't care."

"You remind me of my mother."

"No, I do not!"

"Same deviousness."

"I'm not devious—just realistic and sensible."

"Yes," he said softly, almost to himself.

"Yes, what?"

"Yes," he said a little louder. "I thought I was done with devious people."

"I'm not devious," she said angrily.

"You stubborn fool! Get out of my house!"

She left him with furious swiftness, sending the air around her aflutter as she bolted out of the house. This Gideon was insufferable, she told herself and cursed her ill luck for setting up their first meeting. *He calls me the stubborn fool. Who is the stubborn fool? He is! Who refused to stop prying about my mother? Who prodded and prodded and prodded until everything I had succeeded in forgetting started to trouble me? The worst part is that what the mother did has damaged him very, very much. It just hangs over everything. I came here to bare my soul to him—he throws me out! ... Her action makes it impossible for a girl to measure up to his impossible expectations—he expects an angel.*

For the next few weeks, her emotions vacillated from anger to hurt and intermediate whenever thoughts of him crashed through the mental barrier she was trying to set up. Then her anger at him ebbed, leaving room for self-recriminating voices in her head. *What have you done? What have you done? The only good thing in your life—thrown away.* Instinctively she sought to stifle those voices of her conscience. Her thoughts obsessed over her own hurt feelings and fortified her with the conviction she was the injured party. *Imagine what he did to me. Maybe he didn't even love me at all and had exploited my emotions all along. Either that or he doesn't know anything about love. Why would he throw out somebody he claims he loves? Who throws a lover out like that?*

However, an incomprehensible dread gnawed at her. The core of her being began to feel off-kilter, as if something frail had taken the place of her backbone. She began to actually get the occasional feeling that her frame was no longer steady—on those occasions she thought she was wobbling. She had to forget him; she had to find new pastimes. Her old ones—reading important texts and watching significant movies—required the frame of mind she lacked now. She formed a new habit— watching broad comedies, animations and melodramas. In front of both theater and Don's TV screens, where she would slouch seven days a week for her viewing sprees, she would smile wanly at some scenes as she watched endlessly. In the end, these pastimes served their purpose, for she was able to keep Gideon in the shadow that followed her around—able to keep him there. Yes, his silhouette hung all around her mental barrier, but her head had yet to ring with voices troubling her soul on his account.

Then something much bigger began to occupy her time.

#

The wedding was set. Its master plan immediately shifted into high gear. Elizabeth embraced the burst of activities for the ceremony more than she really wanted to. Some conditions feel worse than others do. To Elizabeth, being sucked into the despondence of her problem with Gideon was worse than dredging up more enthusiasm than she actually felt for the planning of the wedding. Though Don and she were on the sidelines of the planning, as his parents took complete control of it, she remained occupied.

The wedding was to be a grandiose one that befitted the status of Dr. Ihoeyno's heir. It had to capture the popular imagination for decades. Already, talk of the wedding had started to buzz in the megalopolis and beyond. Newspapers, magazines and web sites sought every imaginable angle on Elizabeth and Don: how they met, how much they loved each other, what high achievers they were, what they aspired to … Much of the coverage was pure fantasy. Elizabeth Kōp, for one, had been transformed into a woman who founded a very successful business after her doctorate—she was now Dr. Elizabeth Kōp.

193

With "Dr. Elizabeth" the person to meet at the Sheraton Hotel merry session to introduce the groom and bridegroom to the 150 or so of the wedding planners, she got more contacts than she could handle. Her cell phone—acquired at the behest of Dr. Ihoeyno, who bought it and supplied her a stipend for charge cards—buzzed so frequently she put it on silent mode and answered calls from only a few, including the old man, Don, and his mother. When the make-up people called her for an update or casual comment, she stared at their numbers on her phone and let it take a message. She did so as well when she got calls from the hair stylists, the wedding dress stylists, the decorators, and sundry other wedding professionals who seemed to have waited too long to release their pent-up energies in planning the wedding. Out of courtesy, she returned some of the calls, for she recognized the callers' polite impulses to—as the local lingo would have it—"carry her along." They knew that the wedding only had to replicate the grand design in Dr. and Mrs. Ihoeyno's minds and that every detail (small or granular) better contribute to their vision of that ceremony. But at times humans in CDKuru too, especially the poor, were nice to each other without ulterior motives—just nice. Elizabeth recognized that in the callers and reciprocated.

The photographer, the bland one, re-emerged. He had no need to hide his trade tool now. He had no need to sneak around to snap pictures of his two unwitting subjects in their private moments. He had no need to be paparazzo. Now with the acquiescence of Don and Elizabeth, he could complete what he started months ago, even before she recognized him in a crowd as a photographer who seemed to be taking pictures of them.

His contract was to build a portfolio of the couple from

courtship to wedding. So far he had captured the two on film in numerous locations and on different occasions even prior to the marriage proposal. When he displayed his work, Elizabeth was shocked both by the extent of the man's work and by Dr. Ihoeyno's genius at anticipating the marriage. A question kept repeating itself in her mind. *How did he know I would marry Don? How did he know I ...* Apparently Don himself hadn't been trusted with word of the secret mission, for it surprised him too and made him shout angrily at the photographer for lying to them months ago. At the time, Elizabeth had reported seeing the man previously at an eatery, and they had asked him why he was photographing them. He had said something then that eased their minds. Today he replied, "I didn't lie. I just said that people shouldn't imagine the worst."

"But this is our picture in that restaurant," Don shouted again.

"It wasn't taken that day. My boy had to get it another time."

"But why didn't you tell me when I asked?"

"I have to survive. I was paid to do it as a hush job."

The two had forgiven the surreptitious snapping of their pictures since no harm had come from it. Now it even seemed worth the trouble because the pictures caught their sincere moods at various locations, though the man would have preferred their sunny disposition in all the pictures. "You two made it hard for me," he complained. "See how gloomy my spread looks. You two never smiled."

Now they had to offer his lenses smiling faces. He had taken the two to various locations in the city for a series of photo sessions. Both of them would pack clothes in a car, drive to a location, and start posing for the camera as it flashed while the photographer directed them to smile … look this way but don't forget each other … give each other a faraway look but don't forget the camera … make it a dreamy look … make it a "lovey-dovey look. "Where is the smile?" he would ask when their smiles waned from tiredness. From that location, they went to another of his scouted locations, dressed anew, and posed for his camera.

Thereafter, he plunged them into a whirlwind tour of photographing them as if commissioned to amass overwhelming evidence that the couple was an enduring incarnate of love—CDKuru's Romeo and Juliet. They started with the "local" haunts, the tourist attractions flung in different parts of the country. They touched down in Ajuba for the scenery at Lanoitan Assembly Complex, Osa Rock, NBC Headquarters, Lanoitan Mosque, Lanoitan Christian Centre, Rednow Land, and Muinnellim Park; taxied down at Abokay for the scenery at the nearby game reserve; and cruised to Rabalac for the background of the nearby ranch resort. They looked not a tad worse or tired in the pictures because their 1,120-square-foot private jet had an entertainment center, a well-stocked bar, a well-laid dining table with aromatic cuisines, and a lounge with huge leather seats and settees on which one could spread out and catnap in a comfortable position without being a nuisance to the other passengers. The two availed themselves of the foods, the drinks, the naps, and the movies or music videos playing continuously on a big flat screen in the lounge. Elizabeth also availed herself of the opportunity to retreat to either the dining area or the spacious bathroom to surf the Internet or browse through magazines. These conveniences, with nights spent here and there in hotel suites, helped make the two feel and look rested.

Then the second leg of photographing them commenced right after they returned to CDKuru. They jetted off to Paris, London, Rome, Dubai, and South Africa. Their itinerary again mimicked a tourist package—Eiffel Tower, Place de la Concorde, Arc de Triomphe, Louvre, Big Ben, Buckingham Palace, Millennium Footbridge, British Museum, Colosseo, Monumento a Vittorio Emanuele 11, Fontana di Trevi, Pantheon, Burj Khalifa, Burj al Arab, Ski Dubai, Dubai Mall, Wild Wadi Water Park, Table Mountain, Cape Winelands, Union Buildings, Gold Reef City, and Mandela Square. It wouldn't do for them to crisscross the national airspace in a 1,120-square-foot private jet and traverse the world in it too. They needed an upgrade, and they got it. This private jet was the 4,786-square-foot one customized for an insecure rich man.

The lounges, the bedrooms, the office, the conference room, the kitchen, and even the restrooms flaunted neither beauty nor comfort—they flaunted extravagant costs and extraordinary narcissism. One look at the gold faucets, gold handlebars for the showers, gold trims around tables, intricate and elaborate crests on all seats, and suede-covered ceiling and you knew that an inordinate sum was spent here to make you know that an inordinate sum was spent here. Elizabeth had to pause at the wretched excess that somebody had wasted a fortune on. But she ignored all that and enjoyed the jet's large space, her king-sized bed, and the refrigerator and wine cooler that catered to her newly acquired taste for chilled bubbly. She found other aspects of the jet useful for escaping her occasional moodiness, an affliction she developed after the breakup and usually suffered from when bored or idle.

The long flights would have spelled disaster for somebody in her mood. But the jet helped Elizabeth mask all that. The far-flung lounges allowed her when bored with Don to escape to the other lounge, which the chef, personal assistant, and two domestic staff kept agog with rumors, news, and gossips about any actor or actress in a movie playing there. The large conference room also helped her. It was located far enough for her to escape into browsing the Internet without distraction yet accessible enough that no one could accuse her of being aloof. Hiding away in the bedroom suite much of the time would have opened her up to that accusation. But no, Dr. Elizabeth was one of them.

Once they arrived at a destination, Photographer became a general. Gone were his in-flight subservient manners toward Don. The "yes sir" to everything stopped on landing. Photographer had chosen all the landmarks for the sceneries of all the photographs. Either he'd done extraordinary research or he'd been to those places before, for he knew exactly where to position the two models to capture the landmark in their background or foreground. In Dubai, he guided the drivers of the entourage to an exact location on the beach that had a great view of Burj al Arab in the background. In Rome, he got them directly to the right spot across the street to capture Collosseo in the background of his subjects. In Johannesburg, he brought them to the foot of Mandela's statue in Sandton with the sureness of a tourist guide. Only once did his knowledge or experience fail him: He had done well in London to lead his group to Buckingham Palace and other places until they arrived at Trafalgar Square. For a few moments, he looked stunned and defeated. Then he shouted at no one in particular: "Without all the pigeons, how can anyone know we took the pictures here?"

Otherwise, he had scouted his locations extremely well and had led Don and Elizabeth to numerous global iconic places in two-plus weeks without much resistance. In fact, only twice did he get any resistance during the entire trip. Both times—at Notre Dame and at Basilica di San Pietro—stress had streaked to Elizabeth's scalp, kneading it and aching it until her face turned sullen, and she would not pose near a church!

#

When they returned to CDKuru, Elizabeth met two surprises. One, Dr. Ihoeyno had installed her in a castle about three miles from his house. Two, her expectations that the photo sessions would pause until the day of the wedding failed to materialize. She had hardly put down her luggage and tried to know the lay of the whole house when the photographer resumed his pursuits. He wanted the couple in front of Lanoitan Theatre, Lanoitan Stadium, Awkat Beach and every other major or minor attraction in CDKuru. Eventually, they covered many sides of various beaches and ended up one day at Motorboat Club in Iyoki marina, where he had them change seven times to pose in two restaurants, in three bars, on a deck, and on a large boat swaying ever so slightly in the serene lagoon.

Around four that evening, the trio stood under a leafy tree in front of the club as the photographer tried to schedule even more sessions in the coming days. For a moment, Elizabeth's churning mind hung a pensive look on her face as she stared in the direction they had come from. The panorama of their location—the jetty with anchored motorboats, the lagoon with jet skiers and cruising motorboats, and the skyscrapers on the other side of the lagoon—began to fade from her perception.

She was concerned about something else. Then she turned to the photographer. "My jaw has started to ache," she said gently. "I am not an actress or a model."

"It would be over soon," he said with a reassuring smile.

"It's already over for me," she affirmed.

That ended it, for when Dr. Ihoeyno heard of it, he jovially told the photographer, "I can understand milking this project to the last drop, but the cash cow has to be kept alive."

Though the photo sessions had gone on too long for Elizabeth, they had kept her busy at least, leaving her willfully disengaged from two issues that had been accruing at the back of her mind. Now, suddenly idle and solitary, she found herself no longer able to escape her sentiments about her new house and her forthcoming marriage to Don. She began to explore the house and ventured past the vicinity she'd previously quarantined herself in—the vicinity of the first suite and the entrance hall.

"We take great care of our own," Dr. Ihoeyno had intoned when he moved her into the house. Elizabeth had sensed that the house was big—now, on stepping deeper into the place, she found it mammoth with sky-high coffered ceilings and gigantic columns, more like a succession of halls converted into living space. Grandiose and ornate in search of stateliness, the 15,000-square-foot house had eleven luxurious suites and four living rooms. A quadruplet of sorts, each living room mirrored the other. Each had a loveseat/wedge/loveseat sectional, several settees, several chairs, and a gigantic flat screen television. Bulky and gaudy chandeliers hung everywhere. Outsized paintings proliferated on the walls of each living room, did the same on the walls of the dining room, and left the distinct impression that someone without a sense of moderation had sought to replicate an art gallery in the house.

The furniture smelled brand new. Ornately detailed and in pastel colors, these furnishings made some people remember French royalty in the 1700s—their penchant for the ornamented, the dizzying fancifully curved, and the overdone with inlays. Yes, the uninformed masses had to see these lavishly decorated pieces and bow to the wealth of the owners. King Louis XIV would have been proud that his kind of esthetics, which came to CDKuru on the heels of colonizers, still trended among twenty-first century CDKurienes.

Neither the furniture and decor nor the size of the house appealed to Elizabeth. One was too affected, the other monstrously big. Her mind came up with a simple formula to refurnish the house enough to make it less showy, less vulgar and much less stuffy. *Take half the furniture out of the residence and pry off all the adornments in the remaining items. Maybe, maybe, that would make the place not scream so loudly at me. ... Oh well, I can't even do that. I can't touch such a topic—that will announce that I am calling the taste of the person who decorated this place into question. Ha! A prospective daughter-in-law telling her authoritarian parents-in-law that they have such poor taste. Oh no! Not me!*

About the size of the place, no one could do anything about it at all. No one could shrink a house. Suddenly the grotesque size of the house and its furniture's fastidious style did something to her. She found herself feeling lonely and lost. At that moment, the second issue at the back of her mind conflated with the first and prompted her to question herself. *Should I have agreed to the marriage? Why do I not feel right about it? Why can't I feel normal about all these, not even happy—just normal? ... Oh well, I'd better stop thinking this way. I agreed. It's too late to question a decision that's already set too many things in motion.*

CHAPTER 17

A house intended to dazzle her as just one of the fantastic prizes of being married into the family had sent her questioning herself about the marriage, but that was it. She went along with the things that her decision had set in motion and tried to keep the place alive, tried to make it less lonely for her. During the day, she invited the domestic staff to eat in the house, played them the inane royal dramas they usually enjoyed, passed out lots of snacks and told them to feel free in the house. At the first opportunity, they fled to their quarters—leaving her abandoned and trapped in the formal and sovereign air of the main house for much of the day. At night, she tried to get a few of the household workers to sleep in the main house. They stayed there until she fell asleep and they snuck out to their quarters. She decided that sleeping in the smallest of the rooms there could help.

The room was part of an upstairs suite at the farthest reaches of the house. As in the other suites, lounge flowed into bedroom without a door between them. A settee and three seats with ottomans furnished the lounge. The room had a supersized king bed, a gigantic dresser and an average entertainment center. That night, after climbing onto the bed, she realized it was also very, very large. She had rolled to the middle, stretched out her hands, and felt like she was in the middle of the Sahara. That shook her up. She had selected the room because she craved intimate space—instead she felt she was in the middle of nowhere. The huge bed, the huge space around it, and the huge sprawl of the entire place began to magnify her loneliness. Her thoughts began to loop around dreaded topics—Gideon, her dubious agreement to the wedding, the horror of lost love, Gideon … She couldn't stop the looping thoughts; she eventually lost control of her imagination as well.

The bloody scene began to play in her head again. The drip, drip, drip of blood formed a pool and then a river on the concrete floor of the portico. Snippets of blood-curdling cry from a baby reverberated in her head over and over and then perhaps escaped to the world around her, for at a point she believed she heard them from her surroundings as well. Elizabeth felt feverish as if she had malaria. Ice seemed to fill up her blood vessels while her body boiled. She sweated and shivered. The bed seemed to spin. The room seemed to spin.

After a few terrible moments of these, she forced herself to breathe as deeply and as noisily as she could. The scene cleared out of her head. She switched on the bedside lights, rolled out of the bed, and moved to the lounge. Wearing a housecoat near midnight and seated, legs stretched out on an ottoman, she found her mind skidding toward thoughts she didn't want to entertain. *So I can't escape*—she'd thought and stopped herself from delving into the subliminal horror causing all her disquietude.

She barely waited for dawn to begin her campaign to get Big Mama to visit more and stay longer. But the woman kept running from there as if haunted by the place. Either she wouldn't come there under one pretext or another, or she was ready to leave the place as soon as she set foot there. One day, as was usual there, both of them had been talking in a tone slightly higher than a whisper—talking softly as if they were afraid to awaken ghosts in the house. Elizabeth asked, "Why don't you like my company anymore?"

"It's not your company," Big Mama said. "It's this place."

"What is wrong with the place?"

"Is this where you are going to live with him?"

"I don't know yet. All I know is that his father said he has just bought the place from his company."

"This doesn't feel like where someone has stayed in ages."

"I don't know if anybody lived here between when he bought it for his company and when he sold it to himself."

"I've lived a long time in Irnopi. I'm used to human voices, car sounds, human noise. I can't hear any of that here. Here, I feel like I am in a burial ground and I don't like that."

"Me too," Elizabeth said. "I used to think that the children's snoring was bad. Being alone here at night is scary. If I had an emergency during the night and started screaming, no one would hear me."

"If anything starts to happen, call Chemist [medicine vendor]—he will wake me up," Big Mama said.

The advice was worthless and both of them knew it. So they stared at each other to think up a solution. Eventually, however, Big Mama asked, "Do you even know what you are doing?"

Elizabeth didn't answer that. Instead, she brightened up and glibly said she just realized what to do from now on. Every night, she had to leave this house late after the domestic staff had gone to bed and return before they awoke to their duties. Only the head gateman, with whom she had the affinity of being the only outsiders in the compound, would be wise to the illusion she slept in the house.

So Elizabeth began to spend the day at the house and the night at Irnopi. Late every night she abandoned her chauffeured cars in the compound for a cab to the slum to spend the night there. Early every morning she took a cab back to the posh house to spend much of the day there. But after a week of this bifurcated residence, she faced a silent revolt that should have prompted soul-searching. On that day, tired of going to the salons to have her hair styled, she had asked to have her hair braided by Big Mama. They were sitting in their dingy first room in Irnopi—she on the small stool, the old woman on the settee— as strands of Elizabeth's hair gradually became interlocked. The old woman had been gloomy and withdrawn as she braided the hair. She spoke not a word—she just worked on the hair and used her hands to steer the head into needed angles. And the rare quietude spoke volumes to Elizabeth, who became increasingly uneasy as the silence grew. She sensed the whole thing had to do with her refusal to chart a course and follow it.

"You know that place is scary at night," Elizabeth said. "My only option is to live here and there at the same time."

"Why don't you just come back here till you have enough people in that house?"

"That house will still feel empty even if Don and his servants move in."

"Then, why do you think you can stay there alone?"

"I don't think I can stay there alone—I can't."

"Then—"

"But the man wants me to. I don't want him to say I'm being stubborn again."

"They have a huge house. Why don't you stay with them

206

till everything is settled?"

Elizabeth thought briefly about this. *They do have the space. One suite out of at least fifteen vacant ones won't cramp their style. ... Each suite there too has the space and the creature comforts to satisfy Dr. Ihoeyno's wish of taking great care of me now that I am part of his own. ... I might not feel so lonely, so isolated there either. They may even take it as a sign of my devotion to the family.* But then her emotions veered the opposite way. Her spirit sank. Stress raced to her head, straining her skull. Her saliva tasted like Castor Oil. Her emotions had vetoed the suggestion of staying briefly with her prospective in-laws. Without elaborating, she simply said, "I can't."

Had Big Mama not been so wise as to anticipate the million vagaries of life, she would have been shocked and shocked enough to drop the comb in her hand. She did mutter, "Lord save us!" And she did find the comb frozen in her hand as she stared into space and heaved audibly for a while. Then she steered Elizabeth around until both of them came face-to-face, eyeball-to-eyeball. "If you can't spend a few weeks with them," the old woman said with quiet intensity, "how do you expect to survive the rest of your life in their world?"

Elizabeth had no answer. But she escaped into the belief that the question's hypothetical foray into the rest of her life made it less urgent than her pressing need to survive one day after another. *I can't worry about the nth step of a journey when I'm bogged down in the first. I need to juggle my life until the wedding. Then I'll see what happens after that. But first things first.*

To her relief, the question didn't come up again, and a few weeks later she got a reprieve—at least temporarily—from her isolation in the cavernous castle.

\#

The wedding was about three weeks away when the penthouse executive suites at the RW in Iyoki became available to her and to her bridal train. Sixteen in all, the suites immediately became a continuum of clubs—a mini-Las Vegas where people indulged themselves fully without a thought or care in the world about the next moment. This was it: This was that very moment to catch fun at its zenith. Cups of fine champagne, fine wine, and older cognac flowed steadily into mouths, bodies danced in ecstasy to booming music, and tongues and hands stoked passions. Some boyfriends had become permanent fixtures there, and this group helped inject the risqué into the scene. But when dances became too risqué or kissing and caressing became too ardent, the other revelers would chant, "Get a suite, get a suite"; the amorous couple usually obliged by retreating to the involved girl's suite.

The main location for this continual jamboree was Elizabeth's suite. She was the bride, technically the host of the bridal train for the duration of their stay there. Besides, she had the ideal space for entertaining—an open layout with a bar for five, a dining area, and a sprawling lounge that opened to a spacious terrace. Initially she'd found herself on the sidelines, sipping drinks occasionally and watching the scene from a dining chair. Four girls had tried to pull her to the center of action. They had dragged her out into the orbit of their star attraction—a rather ugly boy who wore shades indoors, wore designer casuals, bedecked his neck with expansive hip-hop necklace, and favored the dirty dance. And they had dispersed the cluster of girls rocking with him, leaving her as his sole dance partner. She retreated a few steps; he pursued, thrusting his pelvis toward her. She froze and the spectators roared with laughter. Then she recovered and ran back to her seat. They laughed even more until the humor of that situation petered out.

In their own way, they were trying to make Elizabeth one of them. They themselves had started out very young as family friends, schooled together abroad from prep schools to universities, and idled together afterwards to carve out their own decadent niche in their adopted country. Now a coterie, they had debauched themselves into having no inner lives. Without a task at hand, none of them could last eleven minutes without a distraction or a substance that manufactured a temporary inner life. When they first met Elizabeth, they had casually offered her cocaine with phrases like "Special quality," "Can't beat this," and "Best I've ever had." You would have thought they were singing the praises of candy.

Later, two of them casually told her they'd had affairs with Don; a third said with a laugh she'd dated him until they both realized they were too irresponsible for each other. "Had I shown up as his bride," she added, dying with laughter, "his dad's ticker would have popped." Their light and friendly tones, with a penchant for impish glee, reinforced their efforts to pull Elizabeth into their clique, a clique that included their brothers, most of whom were in the groom's party. All of them had lived the good life with Don abroad before he broke ranks with them and returned home at the behest of his old man. "That old man," one of the girls began to sloganeer in an amused tone and others joined in, "is new money that acts like old money." That got them laughing uproariously.

Elizabeth used tact (she would be a diplomat for three

weeks) whenever the feasting, drinking, fondling, and yakking invaded her suite. She let it all happen and said not a word that alienated them. But she would retreat to a dining chair to stare at her cell phone and hope to be saved by a phone call.

Intermittently the call came, pulling her away to the Ihoeynos for conferences with the wedding's sundry contractors. Before now, Elizabeth's thoughts revolted to the end of the world during such meetings even as she gritted her teeth and went along with them. Now, however, she'd realized that some things were worse than others. Yes, Mrs. Ihoeyno held sway after the interior decorators' slide shows and explanations about their different floor designs for the occasion, after the flower people's display of their samples, after the hairdresser's layout of "the reigning styles for brides." ... Yes, the woman's voice—hers and hers alone— authorized every item for the wedding as the supposed bride-in-waiting remained mute there. But there, at least, she could stay in the midst of action and tune out the proceedings; she couldn't tune out blaring music and decadent fun.

At times, her escape from the girls lasted longer than the trip to Dr. Ihoeyno's house. Those times, the girls had packed off to revel elsewhere and didn't see her return. On one occasion, after ducking into the calmness of her suite, she thought of her relationship with them. *Things are not always what they seem. Fate intrudes and what can you do? ... The girls want me to be a part of them. I want to be a part of them. Yet we can't connect. We can't connect because some things are just not meant to be. Otherwise, I can't be in the midst of these raucous girls, in the midst of their raucous scenes and feel like everything and everyone around me is dead. ... East is east; West is west ...* Suddenly Elizabeth's disconnection to the girls made her miss her rapport with two people now marginal in her life, made her miss the warmth she got from Big Mama and Gideon. Elizabeth felt alone in the world. Don couldn't help, for he and she seemed dispatched to two different planets. She didn't call him; rarely did he call. On one occasion, he had called but couldn't talk much because of raucousness in his background, and he'd promised to call back later. Two days later, he did. He sounded half-drunk; she was absent-minded, foggy with thoughts of how to find peace of mind in the midst of this whole thing, and feeling lonely ironically.

Then, on the heels of that spell of loneliness, came a voice from her memory. Familiar as the air she breathed, the voice rang out in her head. Its words startled her: "You are devious like my mother." She began to sulk. Her alienation from the world became too much too bear. She knew she had to leave the hotel at least for a night.

She did. She shed her high fashion clothes for the simplest dress in her luggage, tied a scarf primly tight on her head, and looked the part of a poor unsophisticated woman. This appearance of a "nobody" in the midst of the haut monde transformed her into an anonymous being, and she suddenly wasn't worth a glance as she strolled unrecognized out of the hotel, past some who knew her (including her chauffeur downstairs). She got to the main road and hailed a cab.

Time was around six. The last bouts of commuters' commotion for the day rocked the city, and the fog of dusk darkening by the minute exacerbated CDKurienes' urge to get home. In the hurry for everyone to get home, nobody got anywhere: Traffic snarled in all directions without an inch of movement in Elizabeth's first twenty minutes on G Road. With nothing magical to say or do to get the stalled traffic moving, she succumbed to a reverie on the back seat of the cab. So drawn into it did she become that she heard just a faint echo of the sounds around her and moped at her surrounding without seeing any discernible shapes or objects. Her mind had glimpsed an image of Gideon—a halo of him—and only a part of his face came through as if a cloud or her subconscious fog had submerged the rest of his body.

A riot of blaring horns burst that bubble, thrusting her into the situation on the ground. The cacophonies of electric generators drowned out the other city noises there. Vehicles remained parked on the road, under floodlights from gigantic residences behind towering barricades. Motorists expressed their frustrations in different ways. Some wore resigned looks, some cursed audible at no one in particular, and some honked at the world at large. Elizabeth pulled out her cell phone and texted their neighbor at Irnopi. She will be there around nine-thirty, she'd written. The message was for him and for Big Mama: He would relay the message to her and not switch off his cell phone until she texted him to open the gates for her. And around nine—after much crawling in traffic and after much fitful starts and stops in a distance of less than eleven miles—she texted him and switched off her phone.

Blinding darkness had enveloped Irnopi. Grave silence was already declaring the place dead for the night. Inside the first of her uncle's two rooms, a narrow circle of ghostly light from a kerosene lamp managed to reveal silhouettes of the old woman and the children: She sat on the bed; they curled up in sleep on the floor. "That's your food," she said, gesturing to two plates on the coffee table that now occupied its nightly spot on the seat of the settee.

"Tomorrow," Elizabeth said.

"Let it be tomorrow then," Big Mama said as she got up and left for the other room. Her "tomorrow" had a double meaning—tomorrow Elizabeth would eat; tomorrow they'll talk.

Elizabeth understood both and said, "Thank you."

The old woman had sensed what Elizabeth needed and provided it. She needed sanctuary for the night. Though she had also come to talk about her troubles, she needed quiet space tonight. Her uncle, however, had no patience for knowing tomorrow what they could learn now, for he sounded incredulous that his wife hadn't sought the reason Elizabeth abandoned her luxurious bridal suite at such a time for a bed in the slum.

"Let's sleep," the wife whispered. "We will know tomorrow."

"Why should I wait till tomorrow to know what I can know now?"

"Please, let's sleep."

"How can I sleep when I don't know if this is a bad sign?"

"We are not trees. We have blood and emotions inside us."

"So? Or was her text message more than just that she was coming?"

"No!"

"So go and find out why she abandoned her hotel, or I will go and find out."

That was when Big Mama cut him down. "Will you like it," she said, "if your wife only thinks of wealth and riches?"

"I am not the only poor man with a wife in this world,"

213

he protested before falling silent for the night.

The next day, the two women huddled after breakfast in the morning light in the first room. Big Mama had taken the extraordinary step of closing the door to signal potential intruders off. Then she sat on the settee to prod Elizabeth with a stare to bare her soul. Across, Elizabeth sat on the bed, swaying her legs unconsciously. Her eyes stared into space, and in her distracted mood, she didn't see the prodding gaze, though she sensed its presence. Yet she couldn't commence.

"Just what is killing you?" Big Mama asked gently.

"Gideon's mother couldn't have been human," Elizabeth muttered.

Big Mama got up, stood still to glare at Elizabeth for a few moments before saying, "If I still had the temper that I had when I was young, I would have grabbed you and shaken you until all the cobwebs in your eyes fell out so you could see yourself very well. But I'm old and matured now so ..." She glared even harder. "I know it is a shrewd move to wag your tongue to call another person a devil. That way you don't have to judge yourself to know what really moves you to do certain things. But you can't run away from one important thing about people: Every one of us has the same emotions that only have to get to the wrong level to make us do things we condemn the most. Let me be blunt, Elizabeth: She was like you and me."

"No, she wasn't," Elizabeth shouted.

Big Mama said evenly, "Why, Elizabeth, have you come here to talk about a dead woman when you have a wedding soon?" Elizabeth couldn't answer that. The old woman waited, waited until it became abundantly clear that no response was forthcoming. Her eyes softened as she said, "I have known fear and I have known desperation. Both of them nearly destroyed me, Lizzy, both of them. ... That's part of why I nearly killed my husband. ... Yes, Lizzy, I have felt the fever of fear, too. I have panicked and shivered, too, because an adversity filled my veins up with ice and set off a fire deep in my stomach. I know ... I know why you will welcome anything that seems like a relief even though you feel deep down that it is the wrong solution."

Big Mama had done all she could. She had spoken her truth and had nothing else to say. She might have thought at this point that you can push the tortured soul to come to terms with herself, but in the end, it is her life—she has the damage inside and she is the only one who can reach it for healing.

Hypnotic silence pervaded the room. The traffic and the hum of voices outside the room faded. Elizabeth heard nothing—except the quiet sorting of her thoughts. All at once, the woe that had become Elizabeth's stealthy companion since the last time she saw Gideon found its focus—and she gave voice to it in a raspy whisper. "Have I been acting like that woman, or did that death make me a monster?"

"This is not time for riddles," the old woman said in a near shout. "Who told you that?"

"Nobody."

"What did he tell you exactly?"

"He said I was devious like his mother."

"And that made you so miserable?"

"I may be cursed but I'm not devious."

"Cursed?"

"I killed my mother."

"No, you didn't!"

"Yes, I did."

215

"Oh no! She died in childbirth."

"My birth—" Elizabeth burst into tears. For the first time in her life, she had opened up her mind wittingly to the fact of her birth—to the truth that her mother died from her birth. Elizabeth did not obfuscate the fact or look away from it. She saw the monstrous and tragic fact of her birth for what it was, and it tore into her with vengeance, filling her to the core of her being with lacerating grief. Tears streamed down her face as she bawled her eyes out as if the mother had just died.

Big Mama had moved to the bed to hold Elizabeth in a consoling hug without saying anything. Words would be useless now, for the soul had closed off to outside entreaties and any easing of its pain had to come from within. So the profuse weeping continued, with Elizabeth wearing herself out. Consequently, her frame began to slump; eventually, Big Mama laid the poor child on the bed. A funereal air—eloquent with mystical messages—pervaded the room, evoking the strangely somber experience that people had only in their quietest moments. A procession of ghosts seemed to be passing through the room in some sort of ritualized silence. At the core of that silence was the thumping of the heart. Elizabeth said nothing, thought nothing. She just found herself opening up to this eloquent silence, opening up to it pore by pore, cell by cell, opening up to this mystical journey to the farthest reaches of her soul.

# CHAPTER 18

Sudden light poured into the gloomy room. A cacophony erupted in the room and beyond. Music players and radios in the area emitted sounds at a supercharged, warped speed. The ceiling fan in the room spun itself at a demonic speed. The bulb in the room glared more fiercely than usual. Big Mama scrambled off the bed to switch off power to all her appliances before the electricity that had just returned with a surge blew them all out again.

In due time, Elizabeth returned to the hotel. She felt different. She had become a different version of herself. She was free of all the strain and tension that went into blocking out the dreaded thoughts of her mother's death—free from straining her mind to con those thoughts away, free from tensing herself to dissolve the negative emotions of the thoughts and free from the cancerous fragments of the thoughts in her psyche. She had discovered an inner calm about her birth—she felt the profound effect that something rattling inside her for ages had ceased.

Elizabeth sat on a settee in the lounge of her suite. The closed curtain kept sunlight out. No bulb glowed with light in there either. She wasn't hiding from the girls nor was she hiding from herself. Her mood, her introspective mood, just called for darkness. So afternoon looked like dusk in that lounge as her thoughts for the first time in her life wittingly raked over the twin matter of her birth and her mother's death. The whole thing began to gnaw at her again. Her reservoir of guilt welled up: Her psyche sprouted cancer cells for a second and gloom enveloped her. She knew she would forever feel somewhat responsible for her mother's death regardless of what logic dictated or what people said to exonerate her. But she didn't feel like she was locked in, imprisoned or trapped. She could now accept that part of her destiny that was outside her control; she would no longer allow it to paralyze her life.

She got up and moved to the bedroom. For good measure, she closed the door. The curtains there were closed as well and no light was on. Now she tarried in the silent room, deep in thought in the dimness around her. Two steps in the direction of the large flat screen, she stopped as an insight began to form in her mind. At that delicate stage, the thought needed the right conditions to crystallize into something she could understand. She dared not move a muscle; she remained frozen in her stance. Then the goose bumps of epiphany covered her skin, and her thoughts flashed with the insight: *They say that my mother died of hemorrhage during childbirth. Breech baby. Hemorrhage. Mother gasped her last breath the moment daughter uttered her first baby cry. End of story. No! No! No! There's more to it than that! Didn't Big Mama tell Gideon the whole thing happened because my father didn't have a job? He didn't have a job—a man with everything his society preached he needed to have a good job—didn't have a job because powerbrokers had embezzled the country into a crisis of joblessness. Then, there's this other piece, what the doctor at the public hospital told my father on that fateful day: "She needs a simple procedure but, sorry, we don't have what we need to treat her here. Take her to the private hospital." But the private hospital couldn't perform the simple procedure because my father couldn't pay for it.*

Elizabeth shook her head ruefully. *People who say that*

*hemorrhage caused her death are only following the visible trail of blood... and ... and glossing over shadowy actions that set the death in motion. And no! I didn't lie to Gideon when I told him that my mother was killed. That came from my heart. Something I said out of reflex. Something too complicated in my soul to explain on an ordinary day.* Elizabeth began to mutter, "She was killed. Killed by the invisible hands of people whose greed—whose syndrome of greed—is the root cause of my mother's death. They killed my father's chances of getting a job and starved public hospitals of due resources. Why else are public hospitals called killing fields? Gideon would understand. He would understand if I told him that those people's hands drip with my mother's blood just as Lady Macbeth's hands drip of the king's blood."

Her solitude and musings ended abruptly. An insistent ring of the phone and a pounding on the outer door had broken through to her. She picked up the hotel phone too late but got to the flustered driver at her door.

He gasped out, "Madam, everyone is getting worried."

"Worried about what?" she asked with real perplexity.

"You switched everyone off. Madam has been calling."

"I needed some time alone. I still need some time alone."

"Please, madam," he said as his eyes widened in alarm. "If you don't call, I will be in trouble."

"You can't be in trouble for that."

"I was scared to come up here and disturb you, but madam said that if you don't call in the next five minutes, she will fire me."

"Fire you?"

"Yes, madam. Pleaseee."

219

"Okay, I will call her." That promise wasn't enough to get the man to leave, and he lingered in his supplicating demeanor. "Don't worry," she said. "I will call her as soon as you leave."

He left promptly; she called. Nothing urgent had come up. Don's mother just wanted to confirm for the umpteenth time the appointments for the next day, the wedding day. But her tone over the phone was grave as if something important had gone amiss. "You can't just switch off your phone a day to the wedding."

"Did anything come up?"

"Yes! You switched off your phone at such a time."

"Just for a few minutes."

"At such a time, you can't switch off your phone 'just for a few minutes.'"

"Too many things. I needed to collect myself."

"You can collect yourself after the wedding. Right now, you can't marginalize yourself or stay on the sideline—you should be front and center in this ceremony. And when I call, I should be speaking directly to you. Or should I come there to help you focus?"

"No, no, no! I am focused now."

The woman reiterated the wedding day's appointments for Elizabeth before ending the call.

#

Saturday dawned with CDKuru's usual fanfare and more. Community gates in all parts of the megalopolis unlocked as the first light of day roused people out of bed. The gates of Irnopi and other impoverished communities had swung fully open to allow people to shuttle in and out. The gates of better-off communities stayed partly open, with a manned barricade on the open side. Day sentries everywhere started seeing more action than their night colleagues did. The buzz of the wedding, which media reports and mouth-to-mouth publicity had been amplifying for some time, built to a climax. Today was the day. Today would be like no other. Today intoxicated with the fantasy of a grand time for all comers—the fantasy of breathing the same air with demigods and possessing bragging rights about what promised to be spectacular and memorable. And in every part of the city, preparations were underway. Elizabeth's "friends and relatives"—a very few of whom she knew and most of whom she knew not and could not decipher how they became related to her by blood or by shared interests—had caught the feverish excitement in the air and started getting ready. The same fever possessed the contingents who had invited themselves to the wedding and needed no pretext for coming there.

Around nine, the city was unusually clear. Smog lifted from the ground all the way to heaven. Sunlight remained direct, with visibility extraordinarily clear. Weather felt like below seventy degrees. This was a great start for the day since the difference between CDKuru's low and high temperatures at this time of the year was usually around ten degrees and nothing portended the high humidity that usually spiked the heat in the city. Providence seemed to have bestowed divine blessings on the occasion. Then clouds the color of darkness started billowing in the sky to cover up the sun and fill up the atmosphere. Day had suddenly turned midnight, it seemed. Indoors and outdoors, people paused in surprise at the erratic weather. The clouds darkened even more, sagging low to the ground until the troposphere opened up to empty itself of rain that poured down

221

in sheets. The duration of the rain was short, but the downpour was enough to overwhelm the city's poor network of roads without drainage.

Nothing, however, could dampen the spirits of the wedding attendees—not the floods awaiting motorists and passengers, not the heat suddenly spiked by high amounts of water vapors in the air, not the thick fog that now made the city look like a twilight zone. Elizabeth's suite was agog with a pre-wedding party of sorts. Cognacs, champagnes, wines, and buffets of Asian, European, and African dishes filled the place with a rich confection of appetizing aromas. The mood was lively, and people talkative. "Short nails, long nails, artificial, real, curling …," prattled on the manicurist, lips already loosened by fine champagne cognac before she got hold of Elizabeth's fingers. "I can make short nails pop with design; I can make long nails scream even louder with design."

"Just remember what I told you," Elizabeth said, trying to undercut the woman's desire to go crazy with nail designs.

"But Madam [Don's mother] paid for long fantastic nails."

"Don't worry—no one will ask for refund."

"But I want to show my talent."

"Show that talent on one of the other ladies here. She will appreciate it." Elizabeth wanted to rid herself of these professional beauticians as soon as expedient. She didn't need numerous elaborate sessions to get ready, though Don's mother had warned that every detail counted and had been paid for. But the old woman wasn't here—she was at home in the midst of a motley of beauticians encasing her in an overwrought, ostentatious image that only money could buy, the same image that Elizabeth's beauticians aspired to.

Someone turned the music up and started dancing. She was tall, thin, and light-skinned, yet the sum of all her features didn't come up to something to behold, for she had a horsy face, a shapeless frame, and an exhibitionist's attitude. She wore a golden mountainous pair of wedges, a pair of beige three-quarter pants, and a skimpy red halter neck top that revealed her navel region and almost all of her puny breasts. She'd barely started dancing when she segued to the music player. She replaced the music with one from her phone and waved the spectators onto the dance floor. "Let's rehearse," she said. "We have to put on a show for the ages." After several girls joined her, she tried to choreograph their dances. A skinny girl with a blond mohawk hairstyle and a gown slit to the hips, however, tried to take over. She placed her phone closer to the Bluetooth speaker to play her own music. Commotion ensued.

"Mine is better," shouted the tall girl as she jostled to disconnect the other phone from the speaker and pair it with her own phone.

"People don't rave in gowns and suits," shouted the other girl, pushing and shoving to reclaim the spot for her phone.

Elizabeth's phone rang. She didn't hear it in that din of shouts and loud, fitful music, but she saw the cell phone light up with the image of Don's mother. Elizabeth grabbed the phone, ran into the room, and shut the door.

"What's all that noise?"

"It's just the girls."

"Are they not getting ready?"

"They said they will be ready."

"A promise is like a kite in the sky. It has no weight.

223

Make sure those girls get ready—or I should get all my appointments to come over there with me."

"Noooo!" Elizabeth blurted out in sudden panic. "They will be ready."

"I didn't mean to alarm you. Don't worry. They know the entire CDKuru is waiting for them—they will be ready."

"Bye."

"I will call later for an update."

"You don't have to."

"I will still call."

#

Elizabeth didn't argue, but she felt for the first time in her relationship with Don's family that she held the levers of control of her own actions in her hands—she could turn her phone off or refuse to answer it if Don's mother called. The woman wouldn't lead a convoy of her minions across the islands to the bridal suite during the countdown to the wedding just because her phone call rang unanswered. Elizabeth placed the phone on the dresser and found herself loitering around the room.

Suddenly she had the distracted look of someone who should be somewhere far but was inexplicably detained here. The reel of bits and pieces of information about the very end of the tragedy overheard over the years was playing in her mind— her mother howling beside her helpless husband, hemorrhaging on the backseat of the cab to the private hospital, and her whimper of death mingled with Elizabeth's first newborn cry. Elizabeth imagined the blood dripping and dripping, pooling and pooling in the cab and on the concrete portico of the private hospital in the course of her mother's last journey.

The old imagery of the flowing river of blood suddenly loomed large in Elizabeth's imagination—she felt haunted. Then her mind took control. Facts that she had known all along but never accessed before came to her aid. *Between 1.2 and 1.5 gallons of blood flows in the body of an average adult. Add about 0.5 for an average pregnant woman. That's about two gallons. My mother would have lost a maximum of two gallons of blood. Two. I have to stop it. My imagination cannot be turning two gallons of blood into a pool, into a river!* ... She strode to a seat and sat on it. The specter no longer transmogrified her thoughts or spooked her psyche.

Instead, she just felt sad and quite empty. Nothing around her mattered at that moment. She scooted deeper into her seat, though the world was waiting for her to get dolled up for her wedding. Eventually, impelled by the need to hear a soothing voice, she grabbed her cell phone. Her fingers speed-dialed a number and it rang many times before his voice came on. "Hello," Gideon said. She didn't speak, but she lingered to hear more of the mellifluous "hello." She caught herself and turned off the call. She dialed another number. When Chemist came on, she asked to speak to Big Mama. Big Mama came on after he'd found her and surrendered his phone to her. "How are you?" she asked quietly.

"I don't know," Elizabeth replied. She waited to be prodded. Nothing but silence emanated from her phone. She sensed she would have to motivate herself to keep going, that regardless of the nature of her concerns and doubts and qualms, they were hers and hers alone to conquer. "Bye then," she said.

She came out to a silent living room: no squabbling voices, no loud, fitful music—in fact, no music at all—no chatterboxes. The bridesmaids had dispersed, leaving behind the hairdressing crew and the manicurist. "Let's finish the nails," the nail artist said.

"No," Elizabeth responded. "I will finish it up myself later. I have to get my hair done." When the woman looked glum and pleaded to finish the task, Elizabeth added, "Time is running out on me."

The three hairdressers took over. Their leader—a tall, gaunt thirty-something with sunken eyes and miniature braids—picked up the urgency in Elizabeth's comment, and her starched brocade gown swished along as she bustled around to set up. In just a few minutes, she was ready. A large trunk with compartments full of hairdressing materials lay open on the dining table as the assistants and she hovered over their client, each of them with a comb, ready to braid an assigned section of Elizabeth's hair in cornrows. "Your hair is wonderful," one of them said. "Natural too." The other two concurred as Elizabeth murmured her thanks after sighing that the wonderful and natural hair had to be buried and thus concealed as if she had a patchwork of hair and bald spots on her head.

"Don't worry," said the leader. "We will give you a grand hairdo." They commenced and soon six hands were braiding hair on the crown, sides, and back of Elizabeth's head all at once—six nifty hands. They braided the hair into intricate cornrows, moving around her when they needed a different part of her head while she sat still. Oh no! Braided hair would not do for Elizabeth's wedding veil and 45-carat diamond tiara. The braids were the mere foundation for something grandiose. "Top notch," the gaunt hairdresser muttered in awe later as she laid out curtains of virgin hair extensions on a pullout board inside her trunk. "More than five thousand dollars."

Elizabeth psyched herself into a pseudo-outrage. *Poor soul. Worships on the altar of money. Why doesn't she sneer about spending a fortune on mere hair attachments in a place like CDKuru? Why doesn't she mutter about the unfortunate situation of all of us in this room? Here we are—all impoverished in CDKuru. Impoverished in an El Dorado! Why? Why doesn't she think of the cause of that? ...* But then Elizabeth's conceit collapsed once the voice of her conscience cut in to tell her to stop pretending. She had to dwell on the dismay that caused her to sigh a few minutes ago—she conceded her lack of courage to push for what her heart really wanted. *Oh, who am I to judge? I can't even be my true self. I love my long natural hair. But no! They couldn't just style it for the big occasion—they had to sew that obscene number of extensions into a weave over my own hair that everybody admires.* A wave of shame passed through her.

Her silent and sullen mood enveloped the group, and no idle chatter came forth. If the workers' fingers worked dexterously fast before to bury her hair under the 22-inch hairs of strangers, they worked even faster now. In about an hour and a half, they had given her the "grand hairdo" and handed her a mirror to appraise their creation. She tried to be sensitive to their feelings and made a show of inspecting it. "Thank you very much," she said to them repeatedly. She was sincere in her thanks, though the object of her gratitude was not the hair—she was grateful for the speed of their work.

Soon as they left, she rushed to the restroom to evaluate the hair on a reflection better than the cramped one of a small mirror, to see the full spectrum of her hair on two opposite expansive wall mirrors. As she stood between them and perused her hair, she turned her head multiple angles to get a composite picture of the front and back of her hairdo. It was the densest mane of jet-black hair that cascaded from an inch below her natural front hairline to her midsection. On one side of her face, thick voluminous side-bangs covered part of her forehead and an entire eye. Her thoughts wondered: *How am I supposed to see now? I have become a one-eyed pirate.*

So elongated and full and profuse was the hairstyle that it also shrouded much of her cheekbones and much of her chest. This style made no pretensions to being part of anything that would accentuate or enhance her beauty. No, no, no! Hairstyles for carnivals do no such things. This was a weave with too much character, a weave so distinct it overwhelmed her facial features to hang on her its own aesthetics. And being so startlingly different from her natural image and so pronounced, the weave left every feature of her face struggling for minimal notice. No one could distinguish her right then from any other doe-eyed, chocolate-hued girl with that hairstyle simply because the new tresses flaunted for so much attention.

Elizabeth gaped for a moment. The face in the mirror was a strange one with the ghost of her face in it. *Grand hairdo indeed,* she thought. *This is grandiose!* She found a pair of scissors and began to chop off some of the hair. She started with a bundle over the covered eye; then, she worked her way eventually to the midsection. In the end, her face peeked out more; her chest and back emerged from the shroud of hairs. She recognized herself enough now that she could attend to the other activities lined up to groom her for the wedding ceremony.

## CHAPTER 19

The noon hour had come upon CDKuru. The sun tarried at the center of the hemisphere, effaced by a translucent miasma of vapors. Sun rays became diffused and a sun that ought to be seen on ground level as a stark luminous star turned into a poor version of itself—into an orange circular outline in the sky. Wan sunlight and heavy haze hung over every inch of the city as if dirty grayish ash drizzled over the megalopolis.

The premises of RW Hotel did not escape the bleak, pestilential look of that noon hour, nor did anything or anyone on the grounds there. The sheen of both the nine limousines parked bumper-to-bumper and the fifteen brand new ivory wedding gowns that would have been sparkling like diamond right now faded into dull palette. Bright faces and brighter make-ups faded behind the dull, funereal foreground.

The bridesmaids did not panic about the dense haze, however; they carried on with the bright and cheery disposition of a bridal train enlivened by more than a few drinks. They laughed too easily, exaggerated their struts, found every flimsy excuse to parade up and down the crescent granite driveway. The limos had been purring for some time, with air conditioners on and cold air pouring out. The drivers waited near the doors to close them for the trip but every singsong of "We are ready—we are ready" was followed by a long delay. Eventually, a riot of calls on the bridesmaids' phones alerted them they were holding up the church service. Cries of "Let's go! Let's go!" filled the air. And in their hurry to leave, they almost forgot the bride, who had been waiting in the lobby for the girls to sort themselves out and then help her carry the train of her gown into the limo. "We can't leave without the bride," shouted the chief bridesmaid. "I need help." They laughed and went to fetch the bride.

Elizabeth's part in this extravaganza was distinguished and distinguishing. The fifteen girls wore high fashion wedding gowns with chapel trains; she wore a diamond-studded ball gown with cathedral train. The fifteen rode in Hummer H2 limos; she had been ushered into the Maybach 62S stretched car. Now her limo, which had parked in the middle of the others and directly in front of the hotel lobby, took its place at the rear as the motorcade started to roll.

They passed God's Road, R Road, and cruised along the eastern mainland bridge. They were at the zenith of the bridge, midway between the island and the mainland, when Elizabeth saw everything in clear, vivid terms—saw the line of symmetry between her birth and some other births in the future. *When I was born, I was an innocent instrument in the death of my mother; now I am about to become a witting accomplice in future incidents that will resemble my birth. ... In that business with Don's father, I will be the cover for characters who are not different from those who had set in motion my mother's death. Their shady deals would recreate, surely as night follows day, the circumstances of my mom's tragedy ... I could refuse that fake position. ...* But she found right away that the lie couldn't buy her any more time because of its senselessness—the position was her prize for acceding to the marriage.

*All right the*n, she told herself, *don't go through with the marriage. Too late,* she heard a voice dissenting. By now, the church would be jam-packed with people awaiting her arrival. Eyeballs throughout the city and beyond would be scanning for anything posted or streamed about the occasion. The media would be fanned out in every direction to capture all and sundry aspects of the occasion. People pulled out of private affairs—not out of public and publicized grandiose ceremonies. *Too late,* she heard again.

They had descended the bridge to drive along HM Road, Abay. The church was a few miles away. She looked through the limo's tinted windows, through the haze. Pedestrians on the sidewalks stopped to gawk at the fleet of fanciful limousines. Passengers and drivers in cars speeding by also favored the fleet with attention, a few drivers honking in salute to the occasion—for CDKurienes loved extravaganza. She turned her mind and her gaze away from them. Elizabeth was calm, very calm, in her gilded wide seat at the back of the limo. A few feet away in front, buckets of champagne on ice, wine bottles ready to pour, and cognac bottles stocked the bar. To her left, another seat was as wide and gilded as her own seat. She took off her tiara and veil and placed them on the empty seat. She was practically alone in the limo, for the driver was sealed off in his compartment and no one could see her. Elizabeth's train, previously arranged on the floor, had found itself pulled up into a bundle in her hand. She remembered her father dictating—and she writing—"'No, no,' Oscar Wilde's duchess said. 'We are each our own devil and we make this world our hell.'" She was still calm when her other hand reached for the buzzer.

"Yes," the driver's voice came over the intercom.

"Stop," she said.

"What did you say, madam?"

"I said, 'Stop.'" She had enunciated the word "stop."

"Can I help you?"

231

"Just stop."

As soon as he pulled to the curb, she came down and hurried away from the limo to try to flag down a cab. The driver followed her a few steps to beg her to return to the limo. A group of spectators had started to gather at the scene. She got into a taxi before a full crowd formed.

"Where to?" the taxi driver asked.

"Just get me away from here."

"It will cost you."

"I know."

Uncountable observers had noted that bad news traveled very fast. The account of this scandalously premature end to the epic ceremony traveled even faster. The other limos had parked curbside soon after, with the bridesmaids congregating on the sidewalk to overcome their initial shock and press their phones into service. By the time her cab got to the front of St. Francis Church, a dense population had formed in the church's parking lot to whisper and pass along the gossip. For some reason—love for juicy tidbits or shock and befuddlement—no one there kept watch on the road for a girl in wedding dress in a taxi.

#

The next day, she reached Big Mama on their neighbor's phone. "Don't be upset that things happened this way," Elizabeth said.

"Better late than never," the old woman said. Then she added with a chuckle, "Stay there till this blows over. They have been marching down here as if they intend to kidnap you to the altar."

"Please, tell my uncle I had no choice."

"I have already told him that, but he continues to mope

around and sigh."

"Sorry," Elizabeth said.

"Stop being sorry. You are not the only one who's been desperate to feel better. I've been there. Yes, I know how everything becomes about how you cope … what lies you will tell your soul in order to cope. Look at your uncle—he was losing himself too. Thank God, we stopped short of being cold-hearted. Ha! What is human about us if our spirits can't soar?"

"Thank you for everything."

"Stop thanking me and greet him for me."

"I will."

## THE END.